C. W Gerard

A Diary

The Eighty-Third Ohio Vol. Inf. in the War, 1862-1865

C. W Gerard

A Diary
The Eighty-Third Ohio Vol. Inf. in the War, 1862-1865

ISBN/EAN: 9783337126162

Printed in Europe, USA, Canada, Australia, Japan

Cover: Foto ©Raphael Reischuk / pixelio.de

More available books at **www.hansebooks.com**

THE

Eighty-third Ohio Vol. Inf.

IN THE WAR.

1862 = = = = 1865.

By C. W. GERARD,

A Member of the Regiment.

Field Officers of the Eighty-third O. V. I.

Colonel. - - - F. W. MOORE.

Lieut. Colonel. - W. H. BALDWIN,

Major, - - - S. S. L'HOMEDIEU.

This Little Book is Respectfully Dedicated to the Members of the Eighty-third Ohio Vol. Infantry. by the Author:

C. W. GERARD,

Co. "H," 83rd O. V. I.

LIST OF BATTLES IN WHICH THE EIGHTY-THIRD OHIO VOLUNTEER INFANTRY TOOK PART.

1.—Chickasaw Bluffs, Miss., ... December 28th to 31st, '62.
2.—Fort Hindman. Ark., ... January 11th, '63.
3.—Greenville, Miss., ... February 20th, '63.
4.—Magnolia Hills and Port Gibson, ... May 1st, '63.
5.—Champion Hills, ... May 16th, '63.
6.—Black River, ... May 17th, '63.
7.—Siege of Vicksburg, . . . From May 14th to July 4th, '63.
8.—Jackson, Miss., ... July 10th, '63.
9.—Opelousas, La., ... September 21st, '63.
10.—Carian Crow, La., ... November 3rd, '63.
11.—Sabine Cross Roads, La., ... April 8th, '64.
12.—Cane River, La., ... April 28th, '64.
13.—Moore's Plantation, La., ... May 2nd, '64.
14.—Atchafalaya River, La., ... October 4th, '64.
15.—   "   "   " . . . . October 17th, '64.
16.—Blakely, Ala., ... April 2nd to 9th, '65.

DISTANCES TRAVELED BY RAIL.

	MILES.
September 3rd, '62. Camp Dennison to Cincinnati	17
October 31st, '63, Algiers to Brashier City, La	75
February 1st, '64. New Orleans to Lake Port, La	5
February 26th, '64. Lake Port to New Orleans	5
March 6th, '64. Algiers to Brashier City	75
January 30th, '65. New Orleans to Lake Port	5
August 4th, '65, Cairo, Ill., to Cincinnati	398
August 6th, '65, Cincinnati to Camp Dennison	17
August 10th, '65, Camp Dennison to Cincinnati	17
Total	614

DISTANCES TRAVELED BY STEAMER.

MILES.

November 22nd, '62, Louisville to Memphis	650
December 21st, '62, Memphis to Vicksburg	400
January 2nd, '63, Vicksburg to Fort Hindman....	250
January 13th, '63, Fort Hindman to Young's Point	245
February 15th, '63, Young's Point to Greenville	170
February 22nd, '63, Greenville to Young's Point	170
March 11th, '63, Young's Point to Milliken's Bend	25
April 30th, '63, Carthage, La., to Oakland, Miss	35
August 25th, '63, Vicksburg to New Orleans	400
September 25th, '63, New Orleans to Donaldsonville, La	75
September 27th, '63, Donaldsonville to New Orleans	75
October 3rd, '63, Carrolton to New Orleans	7
December 21st, '63, Algiers to Fort Jackson	60
January 23rd, '64, Fort Jackson to New Orleans	60
February 2nd, '64, Lake Port to Madisonville	35
February 25th, '64, Madisonville to Lake Port	35
March 10th, '64, Berwick City to Franklin, La.	28
May 28th, '64, Morganza to Baton Rouge	50
July 21st, '64, Baton Rouge to Algiers	130
July 26th, '64, Algiers to Morganza	180
September 13th, '64, Morganza to Tunison Bend and return	30
November 1st, '64, Morganza to White River and return	900
December 9th, '64, Morganza to Natchez, Miss	90
January 21st, '65, Mobile to Selma, Ala., and return	600
January 28th, '65, Natchez to New Orleans	280
January 30th, '65, Lake Port to Barrancas, Fla	200
June 14th, '65, Mobile to Galveston, Tex.	450
July 26th, '65, Galveston to New Orleans	450
July 29th, '65, New Orleans to Cairo	1050
Total	7,180

DISTANCES MARCHED AND DAYS.

MILES.

September 4th, '62, Covington to Camp Mitchell and return to Camp King	8
September 6th, '62, Camp King to Camp Beech Wood	8
September 8th, '62, Beech Woods to Camp Orchard	3
September 18th, '62, Camp Orchard to Latonia Springs	10
September 19th, '62, Latonia Springs to Camp Field	13
September 20th, '62, Camp Field to Crittenden	10
September 21st, '62, Crittenden to Latonia Springs	23

September 22nd, '62, Latonia Springs to Camp Orchard..... 10
October 8th, '62, Camp Schuler to Latonia 10
October 9th, '62, Latonia to Camp Field 12
October 10th, '62, Camp Field to Grassy Creek 11
October 11th, '62, Grassy Creek to Falmouth 17
October 17th, '62, Falmouth to Cynthiana 22
October 18th, '62, Cynthiana to R. R. Bridge 6
October 19th, '62, R. R. Bridge to Kiger's Station 4
October 20th, '62, Kiger's Station to Camp in Field 7
October 21st, '62, Camp in Field to Paris, Ky 8
October 24th, '62, Paris to Lexington 16
October 31st, '62, Lexington to Nicholasville 16
November 12th, '62, Nicholasville to Camp in Field 18
November 13th, '62, Camp in Field to Frankfort, Ky 18
November 14th, '62, Frankfort to Camp in Field 19
November 15th, Camp in Field to Louisville 15
Nomember 19th, '62, Changed Camp 1
November 21st, '62, Camp to Landing 2
November 29th, '62, Landing at Memphis to Camp 2
December 21st, '62, Camp to Landing . . . 2
December 25th, '62, Milliken's Bend to Dallis Station, La 26
December 26th, '62, Dallis to Milliken 26
December 27th, '62, Yazoo River to Chickasaw Bluffs 8
January 1st, '63, Chickasaw Bluffs to Landing at Yazoo 5
January 10th, '63, Landing at Ark. River to Fort Hindman 5
January 13th, '63, Near Fort to Arkansas River 1
January 15th, '63, Landing near Young's Point to Camp 5
April 5th, '63, Milliken Bend to Walnut Bayou 10
April 11th, '63, Walnut Bayou to Camp.......... 10
April 14th, '63, Milliken's Bend to Oak Grove, La. 13
April 15th, '63, Oak Grove to Holmes' Plantation 20
April 22nd, '63, Holmes' Plantation to Smith's Plantation 5
April 20th, '63, Hard Times Landing to below Grand Gulf 5
May 1st, '63, Oakland to Magnolia Hills 15
May 2nd, '63, Magnolia to Port Gibson, Miss 6
May 3rd, '63, Port Gibson to Bayou Pierre 9
May 7th, '63, Bayou Pierre to Junction of Vicksburg and
    Jackson Road 15
May 9th, '63, Junction to Big Sandy Creek 8
May 10th, '63, Big Sandy to Cayuga, Miss 10
May 12th, '63, Cayuga to Fourteen Mile Creek 14
May 13th, '63, Creek to Barris' Plantation...... 16
May 15th, '63, Barris' to Raymond 18
May 16th, '63, Raymond to Champion Hills 10
May 17th, '63, Champion Hills to Black River......... 10
May 18th, '63, Black River to near Vicksburg 12
July 5th, '63, Vicksburg to Jackson, Miss., and return (25th) 80

July 26th, '63, Near Vicksburg to River............................ 4
August 27th, '63, Carrolton to Camp.......................... 3
September 25th, '63, Near Donaldson to River................ 12
September 26th, '63, Near River to Landing on Mississippi... 12
October 8th, '63, Berwick City to Pattersonville, La.......... 15
October 9th, '63, Pattersonville to Camp in Field............. 20
October 10th, '63, Camp in Field to Iberia..................... 14
October 11th, '63, Iberia to Vermillionville.................... 21
October 15th, '63, Vermillionville to Carion Crow............ 18
October 21st, '63, Carion Crow to Barris' Landing............ 17
November 1st, '63, Barris' to Carion Crow..................... 17
November 5th '63, Carion Crow to Vermillion................. 18
November 7th, '63, Vermillion to Camp in Field.............. 8
November 8th, '63, Camp in Field to New Iberia............. 13
December 7th, '63, Iberia to Camp in Field................... 7
December 8th, '63, Camp in Field to Franklin, La............ 18
December 10th, '63, Franklin to Camp in Field............... 18
December 11th, '63, Camp to Berwick City................... 10
December 15th, '63, Brasher City to Tigerville............... 28
December 16th, '63, Tigerville to Thebodeanville............ 28
December 17th, '63, Thebodeanville to Mississippi River..... 25
December 18th, '63, Mississippi River to Camp in field...... 34
December 19th, '63, Camp in field to Algiers................. 20
January 24th, '64, Landing to Factor's Press................. 1
February 2nd, '64, Press to Depot........................... 2
February 4th, '64, Madisonville to Camp..................... 1
February 20th, '64, Camp to Madisonville................... 1
March 11th, '64, Franklin, La. to Camp...................... 4
March 16th, '64, Camp near Franklin to Camp in field....... 16
March 17th, '64, Camp to Lake Tassee...................... 14
March 18th, '64, Lake Tassee to Vermillion.................. 17
March 19th, '64, Vermillion Bayou to Carion Crow Bayou.... 19
March 20th, '64, Carion Crow Bayou to Washington......... 17
March 22nd, '64, Washington to Camp in field.............. 16
March 23rd, '64, Camp in field to Field..................... 22
March 24th, '64, Field to Wilson's Plantation............... 18
March 25th, '64, Wilson's Plantation to Camp............... 16
March 26th, '64, Camp to Alaxandria....................... 10
March 28th, '64, Alaxandria to Henderson Hill.............. 18
March 29th, '64, Henderson Hill to Cane River............. 18
March 30th, '64, Cane River to Field....................... 16
April 1st, '64, Field to Field............................... 16
April 2nd, '64, Field to Natchitoches....................... 5
April 6th, '64, Natchitoches to Camp in woods............. 15
April 7th, '64, Woods to Pleasant Hill...................... 20
April 8th, '64, Pleasant Hill to Mansfield................... 15
April 9th, '64, Mansfield to Camp in field.................. 31

April 10th, '64, Field to Field 6
April 11th, '64, Field to Grand Ecore 17
April 22nd, '64, Grand Ecore to Glondinville 30
April 23rd, '64, Glondinville to Cane River 12
April 24th, '64, Cane River to Henderson Hill 21
April 25th, '64, Henderson Hill to Alaxandria 18
April 28th, '64, Near Alaxandria to City of Alaxandria 3
May 2nd, '64, Near Alaxandria to Moore's Plantation and
　　return 18
May 7th, '64, Alaxandria to Field 6
May 13th, '64, Field to Field 16
May 14th, '64, Field to Wilson's Bend 18
· May 15th, '64, Wilson's Bend to Markville 14
May 16th, '64, Markville to Cooperville 10
May 17th, '64, Cooperville to Fort Taylor 12
May 19th, '64, Fort Taylor to Alchafayala River 8
May 20th, '64, Alchafayala River to Field 1
May 21st, '64, Field to Mississippi River 18
May 22nd, '64, Mississippi River to Morganza 16
May 28th, '64, Landing Baton Rouge to Camp 1
July 31st, '64, Camp back to Landing 1
September 16th, '64, Morganza to Alchafayala River 10
September 18th, '64, Alchafayala River to Morganza 10
October 1st, '64, Morganza to Alchafayala 15
October 9th, '64, Return 15
October 18th, '64, Morganza to Alchafayala and return 30
March 11th, '65, Borrancas to Pensacola, Fla 15
March 20th, '65, Pensacola to Field 12
March 21st, '65, Field to Field 5
March 23rd, '65, Field to Field 11
March 24th, '65, Field to Pine Creek 3
March 25th, '65, Pine Creek to Canal Creek 10
March 26th, '65, Canal Creek to Escambia River 8
March 27th, '65, Escambia River to Field 14
March 28th, '65, Field to Field 4
March 29th, '65, Field to Field 9
March 30th, '65, Field to Field 10
March 31st, '65, Field to Stockton, Ala 17
April 1st, '65, Stockton to Carpenter's Station 10
April 2nd, '65, Carpenter's Station to near Blakely 8
April 11th, '65, Near Blakely to Blakely 2
April 21st, '65, Landing at Mobile to Camp and return 3
May 14th, '65, Landing at Mobile to Camp and return 3
June 13th, '65, Camp to Landing 2
　　　　　　　　　　　　　　　　　　　　　　　　　 ———
　　　　　　　　Total miles marched　　　　　　　1,831

IN GIVING this brief history of the 83d O. V. I., the writer has been actuated only by motives of love and kindness for those members of the regiment who still live and the families and friends of such as were left on the field or have passed away since their return home. The names of individual members have not been mentioned, nor has the merit or demerit of any been commented upon—all were brave, all patriotic; and the only endeavor of the writer has been to give a short sketch of the regiment during its three years' service in the war for the Union.

The facts stated and figures given are just as they were taken down on the field and in the camp at the time or times to which they refer. The comments and criticisms are those of the writer. The diaries of four faithful members of the regiment, together with his own, have guided the author in his work, and, except in a few minor details, all have agreed. The distances traveled were kept daily by one who had the best opportunity of any to know and preserve them, and are as nearly accurate as it was possible to make them. The list of killed and wounded is not given in detail, because that has become a matter of history, and can be found in the sixth volume of the Roster of Ohio Soldiers; and it is enough for this work to record the fact that, out of the original 1010 men who left Ohio in the 83d O. V. I., only 226 remained when the regiment returned.

The history of the battles of the war, too, have been so often written by able writers that no attempt is made here to reproduce them, and, with the exception of extracts on the siege and fall of Vicksburg taken from an essay written by J. W. Short, of Co. E, from his notes taken on the field, and a short account of the charge on " Fort Blakely " written on the field and published a day or two later at Mobile, in the office of *The Daily News*, the type being set by the soldiers themselves, nothing will be here stated of a historical nature. It is only intended, I repeat, by this little work to give a sketch of the part taken in each of the engagements herein mentioned by the 83d O. V. I.

The only wish of the writer is, that the surviving members of the regiment will receive the work in the spirit in which it is given : and, as it has not been written for profit, it is hoped that any inaccuracies or errors it is found to contain will be attributed to want of time rather than carelessness or indifference on the part of the author.

The 83d O. V. I. was composed principally of men from Hamilton, Butler, Warren and Putnam Counties. As has already been stated, when first organized its roll contained the names of 1010 men, only 226 of whom were with the regiment when it was mustered out of service at Galveston, Texas, in August, 1865. It was recruited and mustered at Camp Dennison, Ohio, in August, 1862, and remained at that place drilling, procuring arms and equipments until September the 3d of the same year. While here camp life afforded little excitement, and little was done that would now be of interest to the members or their friends. Enough to say that large delegations visited the camp daily with baskets well filled with the choicest pro-

visions and delicacies that the fertile soil of Ohio could pro
duce or the beautiful ladies of the Miami Valley prepare.
Soldiering seemed easy, and we never knew before how
important we were. Nothing was too good for us; no for
mal introduction needed to make friends and acquaintances
of all who visited the camp, and, the presumption being
that sooner or later we were to be killed anyhow, it was
not thought a violation of the rules of propriety for the vis-
iting ladies, young and old, to embrace us in the most affec-
tionate manner in public or private. To the modest young
man this was a trying ordeal to undergo at first, but later
on it became more palatable and less of a shock to the
nervous system. But these good times were not to last.
The regiment was mustered into service on the 21st day of
August and, as before stated, after being provided with
guns, knapsacks, etc., received marching orders on the 3d
of September.

In the afternoon of the day last mentioned we embarked on the cars and, after going through Cincinnati, a
ferryboat took us to Covington, Ky., where we halted for
the night.

We now learned that our mission here was to intercept
Kirby Smith and prevent his threatened raid on Cincinnati.
The people of that city were in a great state of excitement
over the news of the near approach of the enemy, and it
will be hard for those who read this, more than a quarter
of a century after the beginning of the war, and who knew
nothing of its ill forebodings at the time of which I write,
to compare the composure of the citizens of that city to-day
with the uneasiness and fear for life and property that pre.
vailed at that time. Martial law had been declared, no fire

arms could be bought or sold, business was entirely suspended; all was confusion and disorder; no news was of the least importance except that which pertained to the war and its progress.

On the morning of the 4th of September we marched a short distance to a place then known as Camp Mitchell; halted for an hour, then returned to Covington, and, without rest, went the same afternoon to Camp King, traveling in all about sixteen miles on this day.

Here we remained for two days, on the last of which, we, for the first time, heard the "Long Roll" sounded. This created great consternation throughout our camp, and we all fell in ranks and formed a line of battle, to await— as we supposed—the coming of the enemy, and show him the mettle of which we were made, which, I must confess, at that time seemed to need a little stiffening. The alarm, however, was caused by a false report, but the excitement of the hour did not pass without some laughable incidents. The call to arms was sounded about the time that dinner was being served, and, like all *new recruits*, we dropped the pork, beans and coffee upon the ground, only thinking of our duty to our country:—later on in the service we learned to look out for the former as well as the latter, and before night of this same day we realized the fact, that our patriotism had cheated our stomachs.

About the time the troops were ordered back to camp, no enemy being in sight, we were treated to a great surprise, consisting of a large number of friends from Cincinnati, who, having heard,—as they said,—of the danger that threatened us, secured horses, formed themselves into a company of cavalry and came over to our assistance and

rescue. They had the enthusiasm of new beginners, and the *courage* of the average citizen soldier. Scarcely had they made known their errand of mercy, when the long roll sounded "to arms" the second time, and in the hurry, confusion and excitement of the moment our friends were forgotten and permitted to escape. They fled from the field in the greatest confusion and disorder, and—we saw them no more. As they had neither arms nor ammunition, the loss was not great, and no enemy having appeared in sight, we soon settled down, to talk of the dangers through which we had just passed and the fortunate escape of the enemy, whose blood we were just dying to spill.

That which is of the utmost importance to a new recruit and puts him in the highest state of excitement, to an old soldier, as we afterward learned, frequently becomes a laughable farce.

On the night of September 6th, at 11 o'clock, we left our camp, waded the Licking River, marched eight miles, and rested at Camp "Beech Woods," where we remained, doing the usual camp duties, until September 11th, when we moved to Camp Orchard, a few miles distant. At this latter place we rested until September 18th, when the regiment received orders to move, with two days rations. The march was begun and continued, the regiment making ten miles and resting the night of the first day at Latonia Springs, thirteen miles on the 19th, when it halted near Independence, and ten miles on the 20th, when it reached the end of the journey, some distance beyond Crittendon. On the 21st of September, not being able to find the enemy, we retraced our steps, and after a hard march of twenty-three miles, rested at night near Latonia Springs,

from which place we started at daylight, and after a march of ten miles reached our old camp about 4 o'clock on the afternoon of the 22nd.

This was the first real soldiering the regiment had done. The march was entirely over turnpikes, the dust was deep, water scarce and the weather exceedingly hot.

We reached camp hungry, tired, foot-sore and out of patience; especially the latter, when we learned that a number of friends from Cincinnati had called, during our absence, with great quantities of refreshments, which the disabled warriors, whom we had left behind to look after our property, had devoured, even to the last crumb.

This was more than patriotism could endure, and the war that threatened for a time was far more imminent than any that we had seen while in pursuit of the enemy. Peace was at last declared, and with a word of warning to those who had committed the offense, we retired to our quarters to take a much needed rest.

Our stay at this place and Camp Schuler near by lasted from the 22nd of September to the 8th of October, during which time we drilled and otherwise prepared for the service, which we knew to be awaiting us, and in which we longed to engage. From here we started on the last mentioned date for Falmouth, Ky., marching ten miles on the first day to Latonia Springs, twelve miles on the following day to Independence, ten on the next day to "Grassy Creek," and seventeen miles on the fourth and last day to Falmouth, where we were permitted to rest until the 17th of October. These marches were wearisome and sometimes almost unendurable, because of the heat, dust and scarcity of water. The roads traveled were hard with

macadam, and at the end of each day's march the bottoms of our feet would be covered with blisters, which were painful enough in the earlier stages of their existence, but became far more so as they advanced in age, and especially while in the process of warming up, during the first mile heat of each beginning of a day's march. There seems to be no time when men are so ready to hunt for, and find, the ridiculous side of everything, as when weary and foot-sore, they stop on the roadside or in the camp for a rest, or, having rested, are just limbering up for the day's journey that is before them. The remarks and jests that would be indulged in by these cripples, at such times, would often bring smiles upon the faces of the enemy, if he could hear them. No citizen can pass without answering a score of questions, and a real genuine colored boy would afford amusement enough to keep up the courage of the men for a forenoon's march. Officers, who chance to pass by, are not even exempt from ridicule, and if I may be permitted to give advice to those who may live to see the next war, I would warn all, whether officers or citizens, against ever making an attempt to pass a long line of men at the times and places mentioned above.

At Falmouth we had good times, and the writer can testify to the fact that better corn-bread and sweet milk cannot be found anywhere, than were served out to us by the pretty blue grass girls of that city. There were many of them proud of the name of "rebel," and what made them truly interesting was, that while they pretended to hate us, their kindness could not be excelled, and they apparently enjoyed our calls at their country homes as much as we did. I shall always have a good word for the

Falmouth ladies, for, though many that lived then have passed away now, yet while children inherit from the mother, there will be no change for the worse.

We left Falmouth on the 17th of October, and after a march of 22 miles reached Cynthiana, where we remained until October 20th. While here, a part of the regiment guarded a railroad bridge, the rest were butchering, cooking, drilling, etc., as it best suited their tastes and that of the commanders—especially the latter.

On the 20th of October, we left Cynthiana, after a delightful stay of three days, marched seven miles and rested for the night, and after a few hours' march the next day, halted at Paris, Ky. During our first day's march a serious accident occurred, which resulted in the killing of one of our men. Four horses attached to a wagon containing a portable blacksmith-shop became frightened, and ran through the ranks of the marching men, scattering the contents of the wagon as they went and only stopping when everything had been demolished and they had become exhausted. It was fortunate indeed that only one out of the thousands, which tried to get out of the way, was injured or killed. Paris is a beautiful place, and to add to our comfort, we pitched tents in a grove near by, more beautiful still, where we remained until October 29th. On the 24th, General Green Clay Smith, who had been in command of the troops in Kentucky, left that post for another, and General Burbridge took his place. On the 25th, quite a heavy fall of snow was on the ground and the weather was very cold. Housed up in our tents, and wrapped in blankets, we managed to keep from freezing and weathered the storm as best we could.

It must have occurred to the reader, after what is related as to our own experience at Camp Dennison and other places, early in the campaign, that the young men in the regiment would have large correspondence, and there were in fact, but few, who had not besides their "home mail," more or less from young ladies who anxiously awaited the answer simply to get the latest news from the seat of war. "Fall in for your mail" therefore would cause a perfect stampede toward the captain's tent. One night, when the snow was about six inches deep, the tent mates of one who did not stop to weigh the consequences, urged him, to go and cry out "fall in for your mail," when there was no mail. This brought every man to his feet and his feet in the snow, and as the wayfares began to discover the deception, needless to say, the recreant, in mortal fear covered himself with his blanket and feigned sleep and innocence; for once having been discovered, no one knows what would have been his fate. After a careful search however, he was not found, and while the writer could give his name, it is thought best to keep him in concealment, lest even now, some dire punishment might be visited upon him on account of his hazardous act.

Altogether our stay at Paris was a pleasant one, and when the orders came to move on the 20th of October, we were not overjoyed at the prospect for a change. Our point of destination we soon learned was Nichollasville, 32 miles away, which march was made in two days, a third having been spent in Lexington, thus bringing us into our camp on the evening of the 31st of October. Here we remained and drilled until November 12th, having in the

meantime been reviewed by both Generals Burbridge and A. J. Smith.

·Leaving here on the 12th, we marched 18 miles and rested for the night. Started at daylight on the 13th, 18 miles more were made, when we bivouacked near Frankfort till the next morning. Nineteen miles traveled on the 14th, and fifteen on the 15th brought us to Louisville, where we pitched our tents on the river bank, near the city. This was a long, hard march. It was entirely made over turnpikes, which brought blisters to our feet and furnished dust and heat sufficient for suffocation. The last day's march was made with the 83rd in the lead, and such good time was made that the regiment earned for itself the name of the " grey hounds."

We camped at Louisville until the 21st of November, having in the mean time been compelled to change our location to higher and drier ground.

A heavy rain fell on the night of the 18th, covering the ground with water several inches deep, and driven from our tents at midnight, we were indeed a sorry looking crowd. The water came into our beds while we were sleeping, soaked through the blankets under us, and finally when it had a good ready, placed its gentle touch upon us, around us, and seemingly all over us at the same moment. Those who have not experienced this sensation will hardly appreciate our feelings. Like a lot of ducks coming on shore to shake themselves after a swim, the men would come out one by one, as each was awakened by the " rain on the roof," and on the floor, and after passing judgment on such weather, in true camp style, perch upon a stump or some other elevation and with a blanket over their heads

to keep off the pouring rain, take lodging for the balance of the night. The next morning, as stated, we moved our camp. While here, we were visited by friends from Cincinnati, and upon the whole had a good time.

If I may be pardoned for the digression, some general observations at this time will not be out of place, and will be well understood by all "old soldiers," if not by the average citizen. In every large body of men there will develop bands, and leaders, ready, able and willing, to engage in any enterprise that may be opened up. This is especially so in the army, where men of all professions, trades and vocations, are collected together. This fact furnishes a basis for all kinds of mischief, as well as great good. No exigency would arise that could not be met and fully consummated by men taken from the ranks. They seem to become engineers, pilots, pontoon bridge builders, or anything else almost by intuition. All of these faculties too, are brought into requisition when rations are scarce, marches long, and burdens hard to bear. The 83rd O. V. I. was no exception to this rule. Men were found in it ready for any emergency. The most notable of those who always succeeded in getting the best of everything by their skill and ingenuity was a band of five, who as I have promised not to mention names, will be here designated as the "Big five." They had a leader who never faltered, and when the cry was heard "now there's hell in camp," every one knew what it meant, and no one understood it in a profane or disrespectful sense. It simply meant the "Big five" with their leader were in sight. These men never kept in the ranks on a march, but they were always there when the roll was called. Never missed a calf or a sheep within a

mile of the marching column and were always in line when
the battle was on. Everything seemed to be in league with
them for their good. If the enemy made a dash when
they were foraging they would always escape. If the rest
of the regiment was starving, they would be feasting.
While others were obeying orders and keeping in ranks on
the march, they were disobeying orders, by leaving the
ranks, but at the end of the march would promptly take
their places and answer to their names, each with a pig,
calf or sheep strapped over his shoulder. Whatever
happened to the rest, these escaped, and they furnished a
fair confirmation of the well known and oft heard saying,
that the good boy will always get his pants torn at the
pic-nic, while the bad will escape without a tear. They
will be referred to hereafter, and as they are all still living,
will recognize their pictures when they see themselves
painted in the history that is to follow.

. Orders came to us to move from Louisville on the 21st
of November, and we immediately took passage on transport steamers " Hastings " and " Belfast," and on the 22nd,
with other troops, started for Memphis. The campaign
now began to get interesting ; for, while many of the
places along the Mississippi River ordinarilly are of but
little importance, yet incidents of the early war had
brought them into prominence, and we desired to see them.
We traveled by day and laid up at night until November
28th, when we reached Memphis. But few people were to
be seen in the towns along the river, which were in an
extremely delapidated condition. The evidences of war
were everywhere to be seen. This trip to Memphis, like
all other voyages by steamers, was a very tiresome one. It

must be remembered that the government did not furnish
us with state rooms, but would pack us in the vessels so
closely, that when we retired at night the decks were literally covered, and when one turned over in bed, there was
general commotion all over the boat, and no matter how
symmetrical your proportions when you went to bed, the
morning would find you flat on one side, front or back, as
you would happen to elect in getting your position for rest.
We remained in Memphis until the 20th of December.
Here we began to feel that we were indeed penetrating the
South, and with gun-boats and forts in view, we now saw
something that smacked of war. All sorts of rumors had
been afloat prior to our reaching Memphis, the most start-
ling being that the water in all the wells and cisterns had
been poisoned, and that the ladies had prepared poisoned
food for us, and things of a like nature to these. Inex-
perienced as we were, a resolve was made not to eat anything while there except army rations, and confine our
drinking entirely to the waters of the Mississippi. I need
not state that this resolution was made only to be broken;
for we soon learned that the true way to soldier, was to
take all we could get, and get all we could take. The day
after our arrival the writer and others were guarding a
public road leading from the city to the country. We were
not there so much for the purpose of keeping the enemy
back, as to prevent citizens with passes from carrying provisions, ammunition and other contraband goods to the
enemy's lines. These were not far from the city, and our
orders were therefore strict for a faithful discharge of our
duty : "To carefully examine every citizen who passed
through our lines, and only permit such things' to go

out, as were allowed by the General commanding."
We started out bold, brave and daring, but when a carriage,
in which was seated a well dressed and beautiful lady,
stopped at our post for orders, each waited for the other to
make the investigation. A large basket of provisions was
in sight, but of course we did not know how much or what
was under the seat ; we had even heard that quantities of
powder and provisions could be carried under and within
the folds of a dress. But who was to determine what the
facts were in this individual case ? It was a terrible ordeal
for us,—who were prepared to meet the enemy in battle,—
to comply with our orders in this particular instance. The
lady saw our embarrasment, arose from her seat, shook her
skirts, and in a tone which gave evidence of the truth of
her statement, declared that she had only the provisions
we saw in her basket, all of which, except a nice roll of
butter and some bread, which were especially for us, were
for her family. This was a confirmation of what we had
heard before coming to the city. We were to be poisoned,
and this woman was a special messenger sent to destroy us.
Each looked at the other significantly, and then with one
accord we declined the offer. She had evidently heard the
reports that were being noised about, and, equal to the
occasion, with the dignity of a queen, took up the butter,
tasted it herself, and then said : "Have no fear to eat
what I give you ; I have heard the rumors that cause you
to distrust my offer, but they are not true. No mother,
wife or sister, would feed poison to the son, husband, or
brother of another woman. Select from my basket which
roll you will take, and enjoy it ; for, while we are opposed
to you in war sentiment, yet we are women with all the

instincts of woman. To say that we were ashamed of ourselves, is to state it mildly. We all began to apologize,
denied that we declined the offer for any such reason as
she gave, but only because we were not hungry, but if *she*
urged us to accept, for her sake we would do so, holding it
in reserve 'til our lost appetites returned. The latter were
soon found, and we were glad of the near turn in the road
when the lady was lost to our view, so that we, without
impeaching our own veracity,.could take our chances on
the poison that the bread and butter, which was left with
us, might contain. From now on our fear of sudden death
from poison largely subsided, and we received with pro-
foundest thanks all the cigars, tobacco, provisions and other
necessaries and luxuries that the people were kind enough
to offer and some, even, that were not offered. I must say,
however, that in most instances these gifts were not meas-
ured in a scanty bushel. Of course these favors did not
prevent or lessen the performance by us of our whole duty,
but the work of making search was done later on in a much
more approved style and with far less embarrassment than
at first.

It's enough to be on a ship at sea in time of a storm
or to face the enemy on the field of battle, but the recol
lection of these, sinks into insignificance when the writer
recalls his first experience in attempting to strictly comply
with the order of that day, with reference to this lovely
woman.

On the evening of November 30th we were visited by
a terrible storm for which, this being our first day in camp,
we were illy prepared, and consequently suffered a great
deal. The weather continued cold and rainy for the next

two days, and though we were far in the South yet the weather here about the first of December would have been a fair sample of what would be looked for in Dakota.

The next few days were spent in camp with the usual duties to perform. Many of us went to church in town on Sunday, the 1st, to hear Dr. Grundy, the only Union preacher in the city. He took advantage of our presence, gave his audience a terrible thrashing with his tongue for rebelling against the Government, and the next day left the place.

On the 8th of December we lost our first member from sickness. There is nothing more touching or affecting than the death and burial of a soldier in the camp of an army, and here for the first time, with slow tread and muffled drum, we followed a comrade to his last resting place. At such a time the stoutest heart yieldes to the solemnity of the surroundings, and the thought of broken hearts and desolate homes brings tears to the eyes of even a battle-scarred veteran. While here a portion of the troops were reviewed by Generals Smith and Hulbert, and later on General Sherman inspected the whole army. From this on we knew that we were being schooled for an expedition to, and an attack on, Vicksburg, in furtherance of which we also practiced target shooting, and I might mention the fact that the target was not greatly damaged or badly disfigured. The orders to strike tents and move with two days' rations came on the 20th of December, in obedience to which we marched to the river, our regiment taking passage on the steamer Citizen, which, with the rest of the fleet, laid at the landing until the following day.

17

It was a magnificent sight now to see fifteen boats, all
loaded to the guards with soldiers, drop out into the stream
and float away towards the South. We landed at midnight
at Friar's Point, a town of a dozen houses. Concerning this
place a wild rumor had been in circulation to the effect that
a Union man had been put in a flour barrel, which was
headed up by the citizens, and then thrown into the river
and permitted to float away. Of course this was an improb-
able story for two reasons: First, there had been no Union
man there for a long time, and secondly, the only inhabitants of the place were women, and the man could have
escaped before they could have put the head in the barrel.
But, notwithstanding the denial of the charge made by the
citizens, and the improbabilities of its truth, a false rumor
having about the same effect as a fact in war times, the soldiers sought revenge by burning the town before leaving it.

Thirty-five more steamers loaded with troops joined us
at this point, and on the following morning fifty transports
dropped into the current of that mighty river and floated
along with thousands of souls which were to be carried into
the very jaws of death. A sight wonderful to behold, but
dreadful to think about. We stopped and started as night
came and morning dawned, the torch doing its work wher-
ever and whenever a landing was made.

Our fleet moved on after taking a supply of wood and
stopped for the night at Milliken's Bend. On the morning
of the 25th (Christmas) our whole brigade left the boats
and started in the direction of the railroad leading from
Jackson. Mississippi, to Monroe. We marched that day
twenty-five miles, and halted at what is known as Dallis
Station. Here the work of destruction began, and a large

railroad bridge, together with ties and rails on either side, were soon burned, the latter part of the night being spent in sleep and rest.

On the morning of the 26th we started again for the boats, burning as we found them, warehouses, dwellings, cotton-mills and cotton, worth at least half a million dollars. It was late at night when the advance arrived at the boats, and many of the men, having given out, did not get in until the next morning. ✦

This march tired us all, a slight rain having fallen, making the dirt roads over which we passed very slippery. The " Big Five " took advantage of the situation, however, and notwithstanding the strict orders to keep in the ranks and the fact that they were the first to the boats, no living thing that walked on four legs could have been found the next morning in the immediate vicinity of the line of march of those two days.

The fleet started again on the 27th, went as far as the mouth of the Yazoo River, turned into the latter stream, and after going a few miles landed. We disembarked here and in the evening marched through the woods about six miles toward Chickasaw Bluffs, where we bivouacked for the night, within three miles of Vicksburg.

On the morning of the 28th of December we were awakened by heavy cannonading, accompanied with an occasional volley of musketry.

We were now beginning a new life. We had been soldiering for a period of five months, but had not before been placed in the position we were about to assume. We had made many narrow escapes, as we supposed, had written

home about our nearness to the enemy at times and what
would have happened if we had met him. We had even
dug Minie balls out of the trees and sent them home as evidence that we had visited the field where a battle had been
fought; but not before had we come face to face with the
enemy and danger. A line was formed and we started for
the front. Louder and louder the sound of battle became,
nearer and nearer we approached the scene of action. Men
could be seen going to and fro, carrying the dead and
wounded from the field to the rear. Regiments and brig-
ades were fast getting into position under cover of the
woods, while shot and shell from heavy artillery came too
close and frequent to make our position an enviable one in
any respect.

We were now made a part of the line of battle. Our
position was just in the rear of one of our batteries, which
we were to support. The activity of this battery of course
drew the enemy's fire toward and upon us, and made our
position a dangerous one.

It's of no use for me to try to describe the feeling of
one first going into battle. All is uncertainty, all vague.
One hand or an arm might willingly be sacrificed rather
than risk a life. No amount of money could induce one to
take such chances were it not an act of duty. And yet, the
soldier, too brave to be a coward, too patriotic to shrink
from duty, steps to the front, having summoned his whole
courage to his aid, and with his life at stake coolly awaits
the result, whatever it may be.

All day the fighting continued. Heavy guns were
coming to our lines and being put in position. This was
Sherman's expedition for the taking of Vicksburg by an

attack in the rear, and how long it was to last no one knew. Our position was not changed on the following day. The enemy had a commanding position from a side hill separated from us by a bayou. Before he could be routed this stream must be crossed, which could only be done at a certain point, and that was well guarded by the enemy. At one time several of our men, in the heat of excitement, attempted to make this crossing. Some were instantly killed, while others sought shelter under the projecting banks of the stream, where they hid until dark, when they slipped back to their commands. At one time our regiment was gotten into line and ordered to go over this bayou. All expected to start and felt no little disappointment when the order was countermanded, but from what we afterwards learned it was made certain that, if the plan of sending us over had been carried out, we would have been cut to pieces. Night came and we laid on our arms, as we had done the night previous. A heavy rain was falling, which kept up until morning. Few of us slept, and because of the poisoned water and low marshy country the following morning found about half of the regiment sick.

No more villainous place could be found than this. The men were simply in an awful condition. The dirt was glued to their faces, and, having no soap, could not be gotten off. Fires could not be lighted because of the enemy in front. Nothing could be cooked—there was nothing to cook.

On the 30th we were taken back to build corduroy roads, so that our heavy guns could get in from the boats. Trees were cut down, their trunks split and the pieces laid with the flat side up for the wagons and artillery to pass

over. This work was continued over the 31st of December, and up to and on the 1st day of January, 1863, during all of which time the fight went on, and it now looked as if a regular siege had begun. But we were doomed to disappointment, for the roads that we built to bring in our guns only afforded a means of escape for those already there. On New Year's evening we were taken back to the scene that we had left two days before. We expected, of course, to resume our part in the battle that was still raging. On both sides of the bayou men were chopping down trees and in other ways building breastworks.

On our side, especially, there seemed to be unusual energy and activity; the woodman's ax was heard all along the line. Little did we then know that this was being done for a blind to cover a hazardous retreat. The rain had been falling nearly all the time since we came into the swamp, the ground was so soft that it was almost impossible for horses or mules to walk over it. We had there a large army, half of which was sick, several heavy guns, and a large wagon train loaded with ammunition and provisions. The enemy, upon high ground, knew all these facts, and would they not soon take advantage of the situation and swoop down upon us?

About ten o'clock at night, while resting on our arms, we were quietly called into line, with strict orders for no one to speak loud or make any noise whatever. In the twinkling of an eye every soldier knew that this meant a hasty retreat. It could be seen in the surroundings. The choppers struck harder and faster, the wagons were facing to the rear, the artillery had gone from its place, and everything about now spoke of sure defeat and a speedy

retreat. Silently, in the darkness and through the woods, we stole away. The wagons and artillery were to the axles in mud; with a dozen or more oxen or mules in front of each piece, floundering in the water, men laid hold and almost carried the guns and wagons through the mire. The mules and oxen were lifted out of the swamps and pushed ahead, and all this time every word spoken was in a subdued tone, every act done as quietly as if we had been operating with the dead instead of the living. The boats were reached about 4 o'clock in the morning of the 2nd, the men worn out and sick, but saved from the enemy. We at once took passage, and after loading on the wagons and artillery and awaiting the coming of our faithful choppers, who had remained behind to cover our retreat, steamed down the Yazoo and into the Mississippi River again, landing at Milliken's Bend the same evening. It was still pouring rain, which continued all that night and the day following, and had we remained in the woods a day longer, all of our wagons and artillery would have been lost, to say nothing of the men. On the 3rd of December, while still at the Bend, we buried two of our regiment, who died from exposure.

The following is an extract from Short's essay, descriptive of this expedition:

"Central in location, commanding in position, formidable in fortification, the boast of the whole Confederacy, was Vicksburg in 1862. The advantages given by nature were supplemented by the highest skill of military genius, and the combined product was called impregnable,—the western Gibralter. Early in the war the attention of

military leaders, and through them, of the people, was
attracted to this frowning fortress of the Mississippi.

"It was in November, 1862, that whisperings of an
expedition down the river got abroad among the troops
then collecting at Memphis, and desire and expectation
both said: Vicksburg. The Eighty-third Ohio Infantry, of
which I was a member, was one of the first organizations
in this body of troops.

"The Mississippi had but recently been opened to
Memphis, which was, at that time, the limit of navigation
southward. It was noticed that steamboats arriving from
the North returned not; that day and night the wharf was
jammed and stacked with munitions of war; that regimental and brigade headquarters multiplied; and soon the
port was crowded with accumulated transports. The open
grounds about the city quivered with the tread of the martial thousands, as they were perfected in movement and
manuel, and the air palpitated with the vibrant thrill of
fife and drum. We waited but the coming of our leader,
and we waited not long. All general orders needing pro-
mulgation to the troops, are read on dress parade, and one
evening the order of the general assigned to the command
was read, signed—W. T. Sherman. Tne name was familiar
even then, but as yet the man had not appeared. A general
inspection followed and, not by deputy, but in person,—he
came. I shall never forget the quick nervous jingle he
gave my gun, nor the sharp scrutinizing glance by which,
at the same time, he took me in from head to foot, buttons,
shoe-strings and all. A few months later they wern't so
particular, but at this time bright buttons and polished
shoes counted.

24

" A few weeks later we were afloat on the Mississippi, headed southward. That was no ordinary procession. It extended for miles along this vast continental highway. From the deck of our boat I one morning counted twenty-five transports. The gunboats, low-browed and frowning, led the column, and following came the largest and finest steamers that, at that time, had appeared upon our western waters. We traveled by day and tied up by night. Our progress was slow; for every curve must be explored, every unusual appearance investigated, and, for the most part, fuel provided. This gave variety to our daily life. Before the war vast wood-yards were established on the banks of the Mississippi for the supply of steamboats. The sudden cessation of lower river traffic had left these yards in all manner of condition, from full to empty; but nowhere was the supply accumulating, and after our passage they were everywhere empty. When fuel was wanted, the boat landed, threw out two gang-planks, and all hands, officers excepted, were called to deck. One plank served for the outs, the other for the ins, and in continuous line the wood walked on board and disappeared in the cavernous depth of the steamboat. It is a revelation of immensity, the capacity a Mississippi River steamboat has. We never found any owners, and, consequently, paid no bills. Wood, like the water on which we floated, was free.

" Twenty-six miles from Milliken's Bend, a great curve in the river, the Vicksburg & Shreveport Railroad crosses a large bayou. The place was known as Dallas Station. The bayou was crossed by a large wooden bridge and at the station was stored a large supply of corn. A day's march, Christmas, brought our brigade to this point, where

the night was passed in burning the bridge and corn and
destroying the railroad. Because of its nearness to Vicksburg, it was necessary to do this with all possible speed.
The cross-ties were piled and over these the rails were laid.
When heated by the burning ties, the rails were bent to
render them unfit for use. Later in the war the rails were
also twisted, as it was found that unless twisted, they were
easily straightened and fitted for use.

"In the mean time the main army had gone on and
disembarked a few miles above the Yazoo River, at which
point we rejoined it.

"New Year's day found us in a swamp bordering the
Yazoo River, building corduroy road. The ridge of hills
upon which Vicksburg is built, in its northern extension,
forms the left bank of the Yazoo River. Some eleven or
twelve miles above Vicksburg the Yazoo deflects from the
hills and finds its way into the Mississippi about nine miles
above the city. The bluff at the point of deflection is
known as Haines' Bluff. This range of hills, called Walnut
Hills, the Yazoo and the Mississippi enclose a triangular
piece of land, through which runs irregularly Chickasaw
Bayou. This bayou, in time of high water, connects the
Yazoo with the Mississippi River, in fact is supposed to
have been, at one time, the bed of the Yazoo, and in its
middle and lower course closely hugs the foot of the Walnut Hills range. Upon this triangle, west of the bayou,
Sherman had landed his forces. The whole of this penin-
sula is low, little of it cultivated, and most of it densely
wooded and swampy.

"For obvious reasons we didn't occupy the eastern side.
We had come at last within range of the guns of Vicks-

burg. The range of hills just beyond was capped with earthworks, through whose embrazures massive cannon shouted defiance and hurled their iron hail upon us daily. Scarcely had we landed, before the elements seemed to form league with the enemy and the rain threatened to accomplish what the enemy could not. Day and night it rained, and day after day, and night after night. The low places were filled; the ridges were soaked; high places there were none. We had been long enough on the river to catch the lingo of the deck hands announcing the depth of water as they heaved the lead. This was readily adopted by the boys to express their condition when routed from their place by the encroaching water, and at all hours of the night rang out the calls: "Half twain!" "Mark twain!" "Quarter past twain!" "No bottom!" Fires in the presence of the enemy were impossible, tents we had none, and, drenched and shivering, we watched the enemy and defied the storm. Cooking, such as it was, was done miles in the rear, and the victuals were carried to the front lukewarm, cold, insipid, disgusting. The end came. An assault, defeat, retreat. Twas in the night time; dark as Erebus. For once we literally obeyed the injunction and walked by faith, not by sight, and a sorry walk it was. Commands were given in a suppressed voice, and each one following the squash of the mud and water in front, the ghostly procession started. At first the command, not to speak above a whisper, was easily kept; but as the danger receded, or some unfortunate fellow sounded a deeper rut than common, or failed to get his heel out of the way of his comrade in the rear, the language was neither suppressed nor elegant.

27

" How the patient oxen, thirty-two of them to a gun.
brought their burden safely to the landing, is a mystery;
and when daylight came, and a pursuing enemy came pell-
mell over the cotton field, expecting an easy victory, it was
only to see the last transport swing out leisurely into the
stream, and to meet a murderous fire from the guns of
the navy."

On the 4th of January we started again up the river,
a mail boat met us, and we received the first letters since
leaving Memphis. This brought lots of encouragement and
we felt like new men after we had fairly devoured the
contents of our most welcome epistles. The boats kept
moving up the river by day, only stopping at night and to
bury the dead, until January the 9th, when we landed at
the mouth of the White River. Here we laid up until rails
enough could be loaded on the boat to keep up the fires
for forty-eight hours. Starting again, we ran into White
River, out into a bayou, which brought us into the
Arkansas River, and, after going up the latter stream a few
miles, tied up the boats and disembarked. Marching orders
with two days' rations came. Half of the men could not
march ; the boat was a hospital. The march was toward
Arkansas Post (Fort Hindman), only four miles being
made on the 10th, when we stopped for the night in the
mud, and which, with the cold weather, made our resting-
place exceedingly disagreeable. This was not all, for the
enemy was quite active during the night in sending us
some of their ammunition.—This to keep us warm.

The morning of January 11th found us in line of
battle, while the artillery from the rear and the gunboats
from the front were doing heavy work. The troops and

gunboats entirely surrounded the fort. Our regiment went
well to the right and near the line of a clear field, on the
other side of which were the enemy's works. In this position we were actively engaged in the fight until 12 o'clock
noon, when the whole line was ordered to charge on the
fort. The 83rd being in advance, went into this open field
under a terrific fire. Directly in our front was a house and
several out-buildings ; these were utilized by the enemy,
who poured volley after volley into our ranks from the
doors, windows and other openings of the infant fortress,
which sheltered them from our fire. But the whole of our
line about the front was suffering terribly from the enemy's
fire ; shot, shell and minie balls were fairly showered upon
us from the fort, and I think I may truthfully say, that in
all the battles of the war in which we participated, the
regiment was never under heavier fire, than for a few hours
on this day. The enemy seemed determined to "Hold the
fort." The men in the ditches fought like so many tigers,
and it was like running against a stone wall to attempt to
drive them out. After almost a life and death struggle,
our regiment, with some others, fell back to the woods,
which afforded a shelter from the storm of bullets
which whisteled about us. Our lines having been repaired,
another dash was made across the field. This time we
went further than before, and by lying flat on the ground,
held our position under a furious fire. Little by little we
kept advancing, all the time keeping close to the ground,
until we had made good headway towards the fort. We
were about out of ammunition and none could be gotten to
us. The 96th O. V. I. and 77th Ill. came to relieve us, but
the three regiments were so badly mixed up, that no one

could tell one from the other, and no commands could bring order out of chaos.

This may not be understood by those who never saw a *real* battle but have formed ideas of them from pictures which put the soldiers all in line. In modern warfare such a line would be cut down like grass before the scythe.

When the real battle is on while all try to keep together yet everyone looks out for himself. A stump or tree is always made use of, and under a heavy fire one of the best points about a good soldier is to be able to save himself while he fights and kills the enemy.

This terrible fighting did not cease until 5 o'clock in the afternoon, when, without any warning, white flags were hoisted above the works of the enemy.

In a moment the firing ceased, and a shout which made the very earth tremble went up along our whole line. Our entire force made a rush for the works, and when once in found about 7,000 prisoners, a large number of heavy guns and several thousand small arms. Destruction and death were to be seen all over and throughout the works. The artillery and navy had done their work well, and that of the infantry was visible everywhere. *Our men,* while sickened at the sight before them, were of course in high glee. The victory was a decisive one. The 83d lost eight killed and eighty-one wounded, several of the latter dying later on from the effects of their wounds. The number killed and wounded was one-fourth of all of our regiment who were able to and did take part in the fight. Our regimental flag had eleven holes in it made by bullets, and nearly every other flag along the line was found to be in the same shattered condition. The " Big Five " were all in

the fight, but were not hurt, and got about all the eatables in the fort.

We slept in the woods, and on the morning of the 12th went to the works, and with the help of the prisoners buried the dead who had fallen on both sides the day before. Many brave hearts who stood before the cannon's mouth yesterday wept to-day over the roughly-made grave of relative or friend, whom he must now leave behind. No pretentious tomb was there to mark the resting place of those brave boys, but many a tear nourished the sod on their new and lonely homes.

On the 13th, while we were still in the woods, it began to rain, and kept it up until the evening of the 14th, when we left for the boats. Once there we took passage and steamed down the river, stopping the next day at Napoleon. About four inches of snow had fallen on our way down, and the boat was in a bad condition.

Two men died on the 16th from our regiment, and many more from other regiments on the boat with us, so that the greater part of our time was spent in digging graves, burying the dead and waiting on the sick. We remained at Napoleon until the 19th, when we dropped down the river, landed for the night and buried more men, one of whom was from our regiment. We kept moving down until the 23d, resting at night and moving under cover of the gunboats by day. Two more of our regiment had died in the meantime, and the condition of all the men was such that no one knew in the morning of each day who was to go before night, but there was little doubt but that death would visit our ranks at least once in twenty-four hours.

31

On the 24th of January we marched down the river to within easy view of Vicksburg. The city is on a hill on the opposite side of the river from our army, it being in Louisiana and the city being in Mississippi. The river makes a sharp bend in front of the town, and across this point of land we attempted to cut a canal, and in this way get our transports below the fortifications without coming in contact with the enemy's batteries. We settled down in camp at "Young's Point." The country from the mouth of the Arkansas River, on the right bank of the Mississippi, is perfectly flat. The river is higher than the land in the back counties, and the drainage, instead of being to the river, is from it. Local rains were frequent and, except for a short distance from the river, the land was flooded. Our camp was necessarily close to the water's edge, with a levee twenty feet high between for protection.

Upon reaching the Point we learned that the teams with the tents, etc., were under the mud, and, as it was raining, the men went back to where the wagons were and carried the contents in on their shoulders. The teams got in on the following day with rations, which were appreciated by all, for we were entirely out of anything to eat. The next few days brought great sorrow to our camp. The burial of the dead was our chief occupation. Every day this solemn duty was performed. The levee was the only place a grave could be dug, so wet was the ground beyond. Men fell dead by the campfire and in the tent, and the whole camp was a vast hospital.

We could not drill and the work on the canal was delayed by rain, which fell constantly, and between pois-

oned water and nothing to do, the men were in very low spirits.

New clothes finally reached us, and were thankfully received, for our manner of living during the last two months had necessitated a change, if possible, long before now. Towards the last of January the weather cleared up a little, and we began work on the canal. This was not a formidable stream, nor destined to become such during the war; since, I understand it has become the main channel of the river. It was about one and a-half miles long with a width and depth that could not be ascertained, owing to the ground everywhere being covered with water.

Occasionally, while at work digging, the enemy would throw a shell or two amongst us to stir the boys up, but no one got hurt, and the enterprise was not interfered with because of this. We continued to live in the mud and water for some time. One night, on dress parade, an order was read, giving General Grant command of all the troops, and McClernand, who had been in charge, took command of the 13th Army Corps, to which the 83d O. V. I. had been assigned. On the 2nd of February heavy cannonading was heard, which was caused by two of our gunboats running the blockade, the object being to get them below the rebel works. Camp duties were becoming very monotonous; to go on a foraging expedition was a great treat; but, as the ground, except for a short distance back, was under water, even the "Big Five" were compelled to stay in or near the camp and content themselves with making vinegar pies and biscuits, out of flour and vinegar gotten in some way from the charitable ladies who had sent it South for distribution.

33

February 14th orders came to get ready to move, and at 12 o'clock we took passage on the Pembino, and along with four other boats, all loaded with troops, started up the river. Our destination, we learned, was Greenville, our purpose in going to drive away the bands of guerrillas that were constantly firing on our boats while passing up and down the river.

We reached Greenville at 10 A. M. on the 16th, and after the gunboats that guarded us had shelled the woods with no response we disembarked, and the whole brigade marched about eight miles into the country, and through rain and water enough to drown an army. We slept in a cotton gin at night, and feasted on chickens, pork and cornbread cooked to our liking. The men were worn out, but the " Big Five " were active in bringing in all kinds of delicacies to eat with things more substantial, and before we left honey, sugar and molasses were as common as army beans.

The next day, having found no enemy, we returned to the boats. The water was up to our knees, and to make it more impressive the rain fell on us all day, until we were glad to reach shelter, which was in waiting for us.

On the 18th of February the boats steamed up the river to Cypress Bend, a point on the Arkansas shore, and on the following morning we prepared for a march into the country to capture guerrillas. The cavalry started in advance, and, as a reinforcement, volunteers were called for from the infantry. These were expected to ride the mules, of which we had quite a number which had been brought along to bring in the forage. These mules had never been ridden, and after several ineffectual attempts by the volunteers to get on their backs they finally succeeded.

34

But, with a gun strapped over the shoulders and no saddle
to sit on, to stay after getting there was no small matter.
We (the writer went) started, however, with the cavalry,
marched several miles into the country, found the enemy,
took the men on the picket post, came to a standstill, when
the infantry dismounted, got into line, and the cavalry went
to feel for something to fight.

It was easily found, and in a few minutes the shells
began to fall thick and fast near our line. Knowing that
we could easily be cut off from our boats the order was
given to start at once for the river, to prevent such a catas-
trophe. The cavalry started, regardless of us or of the
time it would take to get on the mules, and by the time we
had mounted the horses were nearly out of sight. The water
came up to the sides of our mules, and it was an unusual
sight to see us, now off, now on, and using every effort in
our power to keep in sight of the regular cavalry in front,
going at full speed. We reached the river bank a little
ahead of the enemy, and thus were saved. There we had
several small dashes from the cavalry, but held our foe
back until word could be gotten to the boats and the brigade could come to our assistance.

The other troops once there, we gave chase to the
enemy, and drove him until night. We now found that
his line of retreat led across a bayou, upon which we found
a ferryboat propelled by means of a rope. This was put
into use, and soon we were all safely across the water, near
by which we slept until morning, expecting an attack by the
enemy every minute. Being disappointed in this we started
in pursuit again the morning of the 20th, but finding only
a large gun on the front wheels of a wagon, drawn by two

oxen, we took that and came back to the boats, which we reached about sundown, very tired and, I may say for the mule riders, *sorely afflicted.*

This is an expedition which history and historians may neglect to chronicle, so I have done so, for the benefit of the volunteer cavalry.

The rain kept us under shelter the next two days, the boat in the meantime having dropped down to Greenville again.

On the 23d we started on a march in the country, and after going a few miles ran into the enemy. He had a battery, which played upon us at a lively rate until notified that other troops were getting in his rear, when he left with all speed.

We followed at a quickstep until we reached a bayou which could not be forded, and rested at night on a large plantation, where we found plenty of pigs, chickens, cornmeal and molasses to eat, and good shanties, formerly used by the negroes, in which to cook and sleep.

On the following day we moved back to the boats, which took us, after two days' ride, to our camp.

Forage was plenty, and our boat was a Noah's ark. Animals of all kinds were there, which had been captured by the men and were being taken to camp for food. Orders were given the officers of the day to permit no one to take anything off, as all must be butchered and distributed for the benefit of the whole regiment. This was a terrible blow to the " Big Five," for they had been instrumental in bringing in a large portion of the hogs and sheep aboard, and considered them their property.

36

But the problem, as to how to do it, was easily solved. In the confusion that ensued just prior to leaving the boat they went below, each caught a sheep or a pig, wrapped it in his blanket and threw it over his shoulder. It was a comical sight to see them getting off the boat and into their tents. They succeeded, however, and, although the officers must have observed the trick, yet nothing was said and, as usual, the boys were ahead.

The river was rising daily, and it became a serious question as to whether we could tarry much longer at Young's Point and be safe, and on the 12th of March we took passage on the steamer Spread Eagle and went up to Milliken's Bend, where we pitched our tents and took up our camp. The ground was drier, but the constant rain kept it moist enough. Here we remained, drilling and doing camp duty, until April 6th, having in the meantime buried a large number of our men and sent many more to the hospital boat, which meant about the same thing.

It was very seldom that a man who left the regiment sick ever returned alive. I think the best way to destroy the army of the enemy in time of war would be to furnish him free hospitals for his sick and wounded and enough doctors to supply their wants.

Orders came on the 6th for us to move with six days' rations, and we marched back about ten miles to Walnut Bayou. This was a beautiful place, and while pretending to dig a canal we really did nothing but enjoy ourselves and eat the planter's hams and shoulders from his smoke house. Yet while here we recruited our health and spirits, and came back new men in body, mind and spirit.

37

On the 11th of April we marched back to camp. The change was not appreciated. But the new vim and vigor which we now possesed and victory, as we predicted, not far away, fitted us for the work that must needs be done.

The time to start soon came, for on April 14th we struck tents in obedience to orders, and marched thirteen miles, and bivouacked for the night at "Oak Grove" on a beautiful plantation.

On the next day we marched twenty miles to Holmes' Plantation and waited for our wagons, which reached us about 10 A. M. on the 16th.

On the night of the 16th heavy cannonading was heard in the direction of Vicksburg. This continued for some time, and created great excitement at headquarters and in camp. The story was soon told. Six or seven gunboats and as many transports had run the blockade, and were now below Vicksburg, and the batteries from every hill were playing upon them; but little damage was done, and the enterprise was an entire success.

We remained here until the 20th, waiting for troops to come up, and on that day went six miles to a plantation, where we guarded General McClernand's headquarters. While here, on the night of the 23d, five more steamers ran the blockade under cover of gunboats. It will be remembered that these boats were manned by soldiers— the pilot being surrounded by boiler iron and the fireman and engineer protected by cotton bales—but when we think of the hundreds of guns from the hill upon which Vicksburg is located throwing shot and shell with such terrible fury right into these boats we wonder that one of the men survived.

38

April 26th we embarked on the steamer Silver Wave (one of the boats that had just tested the enemy's guns) and moved down a bayou which was exceedingly narrow and very crooked. Reaching the Mississippi River, however, we went to Parkinson's Plantation, and landed there on the morning of the 27th. Here we disembarked.

On the 28th we embarked on the steamer Empire City. A large number of boats with barges in tow were here, all loaded with troops who carried three days' rations and no baggage. We were starting for Grand Gulf, and on the 29th we landed on the bank of the river in full view of that place, and only about three miles distant therefrom.

It will be remembered that we were now below Vicksburg and, with our gunboats, had come here for the purpose of attacking Grand Gulf, another stronghold of the South, and which obstructed our path down the river. The intention was to play upon the enemy's works with the gunboats, and after they had silenced the heavy guns our transports were to carry the infantry to the foot of the bluff, when a charge would be made up the hill in an attempt to bag the whole garrison. Subsequent events will show that our plans did not carry; but that after our navy had entirely failed to carry out its part of the programme we used the same tactics as at Vicksburg. That is, the infantry marched across the point of land to a place below the works and the boats ran the blockade at night. Short's account of this battle is here given in full :

"At the junction of Black River with the Mississippi, south, the range of hills projects almost precipitously into the Mississippi, which, with abrupt angle, washes the base

of the bluff and turns southward. Here is Grand Gulf. It is, by position, as strong as Vicksburg, the massive bluff rearing aloft its wood crowned summit two hundred feet above the level of the river. It was really the southern sentinel of Vicksburg, and the only fortified-point between that city and Port Hudson.

"A little above Grand Gulf, and on the opposite side side of the river, was Hard Times. landing. Here were gathered the transports that had run the Vicksburg batteries, and to their sides were lashed large barges. On these were embarked the troops collected at this point. Between the landing and Grand Gulf lay the gunboats. Early on the morning of April 29th the fleet was observed to drop slowly down the river, taking position as it went, until a battle line was formed in front of the bluff. The river is wide and the view unobstructed. When within easy range the gunboats opened fire. The response from the batteries was prompt and furious. The guns were of large caliber, and the background of hill acted as an immense sounding-board, reflecting the thunder of the cannonade far up and across the river and the plain beyond. Occasionally a ball bounded over the surface of the river, touching here and there as a swallow in its flight until, spent, it sank from view. Not a man on boats or shore could be seen. The revolving boats, the puff of smoke, the whir of ball and burst of shell were but so many signs of agents cased in iron or screened by rampart. For five hours this play of the giants went on, and then—baffled, defeated—the boats withdrew. What next? Not a moment was lost.

" Hastily the troops disembarked, and soon the long line of blue was in motion, steadily advancing, still southward.

40

"Then followed one of the most vivid and exciting scenes of this memorable campaign. The march to De Shroou's was accomplished in a short time, and the army bivouacked in a broad plain screened from the river by only the levee. Twelve thousand soldiers were gathered around brightly-burning campfires, sipping coffee and discussing the events of the day, when glimmer after glimmer of light, followed by peal after peal of cannon, brought the camp to their feet. · 'Twas the upriver batteries and the gunboats. The fight was on once more, this time to prevent the fleet and transports from passing the batteries, and now the batteries are defeated. In the darkness every discharge of gun and burst of shell were fearfully vivid. The aim of the moving boats could not be accurate, and from water's brink to hill's summit the glancing shells scarred the rocks and blasted the tress with demoniacal fury, and lighted the dark forest masses with their fiery breath. Every light in the boats had been either extinguished or concealed, and the vessels moved upon the river floating volcanoes, from whose craters·poured the smoke of internal fires. Not a boat was lost, and each one, as it came below the danger line, threw out the glad, fiery signal, red, white and blue, lighting the river from bank to bank and far down its silent course. The enthusiasm of the troops knew no bounds. Each boat, as it threw out the signal of safety, was greeted with round after round of enthusiastic applause, and until long in the night wave after wave of patriotic song rolled back and forth from extremity to extremity of the camp."

On the following day the river was crossed and we landed at Bruinsburg, from which place a start was made

with four days' rations for a place known as Magnolia Hills, about fifteen miles away. Upon reaching there (May 1st) we were very tired and much distressed from loss of sleep. A short distance this side a stop was made for rest. We had marched all night, and in a moment dropped to sleep. It was only for a minute, however, for the roar of musketry and thunder from the artillery soon gave evidence of the fact that Harris' division, which was in advance, had been attacked by the enemy. The order was given to throw off everything but gun and ammunition and double quick to the scene of action. When we arrived at the top of the hill the fight was at its worst. In the valley below our men seemed to be falling back, while the enemy was advancing. We were placed in reserve that we might reinforce our troops if they were forced back to where we were. The fight in front for a time was furious, and it seemed certain that the enemy would press forward upon us. We were also supporting the 17th Ohio Battery, and when General Burbridge said, "Boys, hold this hill if you can, but, if you have to go, take these guns with you," it was answered by a thousand voices, "We'll hold the hill." The enemy at last faltered, then began to fall back with our troops close in his rear, until another stand was made. All day long the fight went on. Our regiment went to the left, right or center as the necessities of the case seemed to require until after noon. The time now come when we must take the advance. The enemy soon got range of us and towards evening turned their heavy guns upon our lines with such fury that we were obliged to fall back over the hill to save ourselves from being cut to pieces. There night found us and here we slept until morning. The air was cold and we

were chilled through and through; but, without fire or
blankets, thoroughly exhausted, we slept, nevertheless. Of
course fires were forbidden luxuries, and the sufferings of
that night were beyond description.

. At midnight there was an alarm which brought us all
to our feet in a moment, and every man in the regiment
stood shaking as if with a hard chill. But morning came
and with it the retreat of the enemy. Our forces moved
on to Port Gibson, where we found houses filled with the
wounded from the day before and the town otherwise almost
depopulated.

The bridge over Bayou Pierre had been burned by the
retreating army, and we were compelled to stop there for a
day to build a pontoon. These were constructed by plac-
ing rubber boats on the water, tying them in position, thus
making them the foundation for the timbers over which we
crossed. Of course, after the army was over, the bridge was
taken up and the boats carried with us. While here our
blankets, knapsacks, etc., were brought up. Also a squad
was detailed to go back on the field and bury the dead who
fell in the battle, and whom we must now leave for all
time. These were not a few, and many good and true
spirits were left under the shade of those beautiful mag-
nolias. Our brigade was the first to reach the town. General McPherson's corps, the 17th, came next. May 3d, up
at 4 A. M., the brigade in which we were was in front. The
bridge was crossed, and on we went towards Vicksburg.

The day was extremely hot and every bend in the
road had to be watched, as we knew not what moment the
enemy would appear in our front. After a march of nine
miles a halt was made and a rest, while waiting for the

troops to come up, until May 7th. These three days were
spent in getting something to eat. We could look for little
from our commissaries until Vicksburg was reached. The
men were bringing in horses, wagons, carriages and vehicles
of every kind loaded with meat and corn. Droves of hogs,
sheep and cattle were constantly coming in. The whole
camp was a butcher shop; meat was plenty, but bread and
salt scarce. The enemy had been twice over this same
country and of course had taken the best, but we were
here and must find something to eat.

May 7th a march of fifteen miles was made to Rocky
Springs. It was a sight to behold: the army moving, bug-
gies, carriages, wagons, carts, everything on wheels, and
every animal on four legs was represented there. The
"Big five" rode in carriages with double teams. Others
were glad to get an old cart with rope harness. Now the
13th, 15th and 17th army corps had crossed the Mississippi
River and were moving on parallel roads to Vicksburg.
The darkey was here in great abundance. He had just
begun to realize that he was free. He wanted to, and did,
go with us, willing to do anything and suffer any privation,
just so he could follow the Union Army.

The troops now must have covered many miles of
country in length and breadth. The movement of this
vast army was directed by signals from the tops of build-
ings or trees by day, and rockets by night. Our commanders were well known then, but better before the close
of the war. Grant, Logan, Quinby, McClernand, McPherson, Burbridge, A. J. Smith, Osterhaus and many others as
good, made up the list; but better than all, an army of
men that had never faltered, followed those leaders. We

rested the 8th, but moved on the next day, making a
march of eight miles to Big Sandy Creek. There we were
pressing in upon the pickets of the enemy, and strict orders
were given to remain in camp. About 10 o'clock the " Big
five " appeared with chickens, sugar, honey and sweet
potatoes, until they staggered under their loads. Of course
they had obeyed orders. They had just come from a large
plantation, where they found supper on the table and the
people gone.

On May 10th a march of twelve miles was made to
Cayuga ; rations were short and we were getting very weak :
meat without salt or bread was not palatable at best, but
now it was getting scarce. We waited here a day, the wagons
came up with some crackers and meat, three day's rations.
were given to last five, but this brought joy into our camp
and filled our souls with delight. The march was continued
with little interruption until the 16th of May, when we
found the enemy in great force at Champion Hills. There
the fighting began in the morning and lasted all day. Our
batteries were playing upon the enemy and in return
received from them a vigorous response. Horses were
literally torn to pieces and the guns more than once had to
be manned by men taken from the infantry. The musketry
fire was no less destructive along the whole line. We
were under a villainous fire until stopped by the darkness
of the night. We laid down to sleep fully armed and
equipped, with a battery in our front and the lines of the
enemy not far away. About midnight the report of a
musket brought us all suddenly to our feet and in line.
What caused this, was never known. A report went out
that an orderly, carrying a message, rode through the camp,

frightened a sleeping soldier, who jumped up suddenly and
by accident fired his gun. It was painful in the extreme
to see these thousands of men, trembling and half asleep,
wondering where they were and what had happened. The
imaginary and real are so closely connected at such times
of excitement, that almost anything may be expected from
men who are sleeping soundly after a day's engagement.

The next morning the enemy had gone, but were soon
found at Black River Bridge. After a feeble resistance he
fled however, burning the bridge and leaving the field to
us. The victory here was complete. The white flag was
seen on the enemy's works, then came a race for the prize;
field officers seized the flags of their respective regiments
and rode at full speed to plant them first on the forts that
had been surrendered.

The bridge over Black River was soon made, and on
the 19th we were on our way to the enemy's stronghold.
We marched twelve miles, stopping four miles this side of
the city. The scene on the morning of the 19th of May
beggars description. The country back of the city is very
hilly, and quite a number of houses were in easy view.
Women and children were fleeing from their homes with
blankets and quilts, trying to escape from the terrible
doom of being placed between these two contending
armies. The soldiers felt the responsibility too. No one
knew what that day would bring forth. Step by step we
advanced, until the pickets met and the fight was fairly on.
What took place during the next forty-seven days, is
graphically described by Short, who was on the ground with
the regiment. I give it in his language :

46

" The whole country in the vicinity of Vicksburg is hilly, and the hills themselves are furrowed with numerous and deep ravines. At this time the hills were covered with a straggling growth of timber, except in front of the fortifications, where it had been felled to impede approach and to give clear view and unobstructed range to the guns. The hills afforded excellent protection to the skirmishers and sharpshooters of the enemy, who, from every crest, disputed our farther advance. To right and left the long lines of skirmishers cautiously took position and steadily advanced. We availed ourselves of every possible protection—trees, stumps, rocks, depressions in the ground—and when nothing offered protection lay flat on the ground and advanced on all-fours, or ran rapidly to any shelter. Occasionally the enemy abandoned an entire range at one time, and with a cheer, and on the run, we made a corresponding advance. At last every enemy had been driven within the intrenchments, and we had secured position within long range of his works. The fox was holed; to drag him out or dig him out was now the question; which?

" The first night, after the regiments had been assigned positions in sheltered places, heavy details were made for fatigue duty. Armed with pick and spade and ax we began to clear roads to the hilltops for the cannon. As yet we had only a few tools previously used in the construction of bridges and repair of roads, for, remember, the siege work had not yet begun. The hills were so steep that to use horses was impossible. Attached to every fieldpiece is a prolonge, a coil of stout, heavy rope, but what its use was I had not learned. It was soon found out. The gun was unlimbered, these ropes were attached, and with fifty or a

hundred men in front, others at the wheels, and others still behind by pull and lift and push the cannon was put in position on the top of the hill. Remember, this was in May, when the blackberries were ripe and the harvest fly sang his note in the trees over our heads. Then, too, only five days' rations had been issued from the time we left Bruinsburg, eighteen days before, and the inner man was making loud demands for recognition.

"At the first peep of dawn the tops of the hills were a blaze of fire and a cloud of smoke, and the garrison and inhabitants of Vicksburg were called to duty by the music of the Union. The day was spent in securing advantageous positions and a nearer approach to the works. In the afternoon, with a volley and a cheer, the whole picket line moved forward on the run and practically took the position destined to be occupied for the next forty-seven days. The position thus secured was not left except under cover of darkness.

"We knew nothing of the success of the works on other parts of the line until some time about the 20th or 21st, when General Grant, unattended, passed through our regimental quarters. Rations were decidedly scarce, and one of the boys, displaying an empty haversack, called out, "hard tack." Instantly the cry was taken up by the whole regiment. The General stopped, smiled and said: "General Sherman has captured Haine's Bluff and opened communications with our fleet, and we shall have plenty of supplies in a day or two." This information was greeted with such cheers as seldom falls on the ears of mortals, and it evidently impressed the great captain, for this is one of the few incidents he narrates in his memoirs. * *

48

" The 22nd came, the day of the assault. The troops were massed in sheltered places as quietly and unobservedly as possible. Most of the artillery had, by this time, been placed in position, and, at the signal, two hundred guns belched forth hoarse thunder. The startled hills trembled to their foundations. The flight of rifled ball cut the air with horrid screech, and gun and shell polluted all the atmosphere with sulphurous breath, whose fumes rose like exhalations from the infernal pit. For twenty minutes the storm raged, and then there was a silence so still—no, language fails; imagination is powerless; it could be felt but not described. Men felt the impress of the Invisible, for eternity lay between the foot and the top of that hill. 'Twas but a minute. The line dressed, the command was given, and, elbow to elbow, that thirteen miles of blue moved toward the Confederate works. We reached them; that was all. Those massive redoubts and miles of rifle pits had not been built to turn over, with slight resistance, into the hands of an enemy. Every embrasure and every foot of rifle pit blazed and smoked and hissed, and hurled volleys of multitudinous death. We reached the brow of the hill and threw ourselves flat upon the ground to escape the withering fire from the trenches. A few reached the ditch in front of the fort, and were rescued only by digging a trench to the ditch from the brow of the hill. We were so close to the enemy's works that from the front he overlooked us, and threw hand grenades into our ranks, while a murderous fire from a hill to our right enfiladed us and depleted our ranks. For ten mortal hours we lay upon the brow of that hill in the scorching sun of an unclouded summer day. Right and left, pale and blanched, stretched out

upon the green sward, lay the forms of our comrades heedless of the storm that raged about them. Twilight came, but the conflict ended not until darkness settled down over the hills and the stars one by one silently took their stations in the blue vault above. Then we withdrew and left the field to the enemy and to the dead.

"From the horrors of that night I shall not lift the vail. Under a flag of truce we buried our dead a day or two later, and then the murderous work went on.

"Then began the work of the siege. We made ourselves as comfortable as possible on the hillsides; built roads for the supply trains, and took turns at handling guns by day and spades and picks by night. Earthworks rose as by magic. At first a line of mere rifle pits was drawn around the enemy; then forts with heavy redoubts, linked together by lighter works, so that, from one end of the line to the other one could pass with little danger. The guns of the enemy were absolutely silenced. Early one morning a solid shot from the garrison went crashing through the treetops away to the rear. Every gun on our line within reach was turned on that indiscreet cannon, and in a few minutes by actual count over forty shells and balls dropped into its vicinity. It maintained an ominous silence thereafter.

"In places where the two lines of works were remote pickets were stationed after dark and withdrawn before day; at all other places the rifle pits were the picket line, and they blazed and smoked incessantly with the discharge of musketry. Sharpshooting became a fine art, and ill fared the man, Johnny or Yank, who exposed himself.

50

"Not three hundred yards from where we one day were on the line the Johnnies were noticed repairing their earthworks. Our musketry fire directed to that point produced no effect, but a well-directed shell lodged in the very spot, raised the earthwork skyward and a cheer at the same time from our trenches. On the day of surrender we learned that the working party was so completely buried that it had to be dug out.

"But let us view the line by night. Take your stand with me on yonder hill. It isn't safe. but we'll take chances. To the left the line is obscured, but to the right. stretching away for miles, are the rifle pits, blazing with musketry, and on yon summit stand Fort Hill and the opposing works, fringed with the gleam and sparkle of combat. Look! in the west is a faint flash, a mere glimmer as of lightning below the horizon, followed by a report of distant thunder. And, see! there shoots above the hill a point of light like a meteor going heavenward. Up, up, up, with graceful curve, it goes, and now it pauses just an instant in mid-air and turns earthward, and, listen! the air is troubled, and shivers with the whir of rushing pinions, and the shiver deepens to a roar like the mad fury of an on-coming cyclone, and the point of light glares like the eye of a demon, and now it bursts with hideous combustion, and the shout of the liberated spirit fills the great vault above and sends a tremor through the everlasting hills. 'Tis the mortar's " red glare painting hell on the sky."

"As soon as the earthworks afforded protection and were sufficiently strong, saps were sunk under the principal forts of the enemy. This work was pushed forward day

and night, and toward the last the sound of the enemy's picks, was plainly heard, as he countermined to intercept us.

"One of the strongest points on the enemy's line, and, from our position, the highest in view, was Fort Hill. It was in front of General Logan's division, and here the first mine was successfully constructed. When ready to be exploded the troops along the entire front were massed in the trenches to prevent the concentration of the enemy, and to render assistance should any advantage be gained. It was in the afternoon; the tremor of the exploded mine was felt for miles; the solid ramparts surged outward, and a massive dusty cone, mingled with smoke, rose in air, followed by the thunder-clap of the liberated force. Instantly every cannon sent its iron compliments inside the intrenchments, backed by a rousing cheer from the investing battalions. No special advantage was gained and no assault was attempted.

"As soon as the siege work was fairly under way every regiment was assigned a definite place in line of battle upon the crest of the range of hills, and in case of a night alarm every man repaired at once to his place. Day and night the firing in the trenches was uniform, a little less or a little more attracting instant attention. As the clutch of hunger gripped tighter and tighter upon the garrison more stringent precautions were taken against night surprises. Sometimes we lay upon our arms in line of battle until midnight, then retiring to our quarters. One night, when unusual fear was entertained, we were massed for several hours in the narrow valleys and ravines, awaiting and expecting an attempt to break through our line. * *

52

"Occasionally we held interviews with the Johnnies between the picket lines. Coffee, for which they made prodigal offers of tobacco, was in demand, in fact, tobacco and mule meat were the only things they had to offer, and toward the last the mules failed them. These interviews took place in the dusk of the evening, and in no case was there a violation of confidence. Upon that part of the line where the agreement was made the firing ceased and was resumed only when both parties called out "all right" or "resume firing," when the rifle pits blazed as before. Toward the last of the siege these interviews were prohibited.

"For weeks the experiences were the same. June went, July came. The trenches and approaches had been deepened and widened until four men could march abreast or a field-piece could be moved from point to point unobserved.

"On the 3d of July I was returning from picket duty some miles in the rear, and approaching our lines noticed that the rifle pits were silent and the usual lounging places deserted. Nearing the camp of the 48th Ohio Infantry I saw that the men were drawn up in line listening to the reading of an order. The order conveyed the intelligence that Pemberton had made overtures for surrender; that negotiations were then pending; that they would probably result in capitulation; that, in any event, the end was near; signed, U. S. Grant.

"The silent picket lines were explained, and, with the knowledge, what a sense of infinite relief; for we felt sure that Pemberton would not take the risk of a Fourth of July assault; and every preparation indicated an assault soon; and everyone believed it would be next day.

53

"The strokes of the town clock rang out that night with unusual distinctness. The morning of the Fourth came. Still quiet. Ten o'clock, and upon every Confederate fort white flags appeared. Our skirmishers laid down their guns and stood erect upon our works. The hills and long lines of earthworks everywhere seemed covered with blue. Not a cheer was heard. Strict quiet reigned supreme."

It was hard indeed that after a siege of this kind, the army that had so long waited for what had now come, could not march triumphantly into the city. But such was the case. Our lines were formed just outside of the enemy's works and he came out in full force, stacked arms in front of us and the soldiers retired to the forts. A strong guard was placed between us and the city and no one permitted to pass. This, of course, did not prevent all from going in and many of us worked our way through the bushes, past the guards and into the city some time before General Grant and staff got there. The scene from the hill above the landing on that day was one that the writer will not soon forget. The flagship landed at the wharf, and about the same time General Grant and staff, with a large number of other officers, rode up in full uniform and went aboard the boat. These were received by Admiral Porter and his men with naval honors. How the victory was celebrated inside the boat I am unable to state, but the reader may draw his own conclusions. The only surprise that I experienced, was the absence of the "Big five" from the festivities on that occasion. They were not there. Our stay had to be short, however, as orders had already come to move on to Jackson, Miss., at once. The town was badly riddled with

shot and shell, people were living in holes dug in the hillsides and the soldiers were nearly starved for want of
something to eat. We had plenty now, and it was not
long until our men were dividing their meat and crackers
with the very men they had been so fiercely fighting for
more than two months. We found here about 27,000
prisoners, 150 large and many thousand small guns.

In obedience to the order before given, we started on
the 5th of July for Jackson, Miss. The weather was fearfully hot and sunstrokes were frequent. This march lasted
until July 10th. We had plenty to eat and except for the
hot weather, a good time. Once more we could stand erect.
For months we had almost feared to raise our heads above
our knees, as we never knew but what some one was taking
aim at us from an unseen quarter. The "Big five" were
now at their best. A horse and wagon had been pressed
into service, and loads of corn, pork, etc., came into camp
at every stop. They had been compelled to remain in
camp while the seige was in progress and now worked with
renewed energy. Of course they had passed through the
last engagement unhurt, and they often proved a blessing
to others, for they divided their foraged provisions with
those who were more timid and feared to disobey orders.

On the 10th cannonading was heard in our front. On
the 11th the fight began in earnest. We could now see the
courthouse at Jackson. On the 12th and 13th charges and
countercharges were made and many were killed. We
threw up breastworks for protection as we moved forward.
On the 14th a flag of truce was sent to our lines, the
enemy asking for a cessation of hostilities until the dead
could be buried. On the 15th we rested while works were

being built all along the line. The "Big five" went out
with their wagon and brought in a load of vegetables, and
we feasted for a time right under the guns of the enemy.

The next two days were spent in skirmishing along
the whole line ; the pickets of the contending armies were
so close together, that at night time a stone or stick would
sometimes drop within our lines. On the night of the 17th
work seemed to be going on in the enemy's camp and
bands played as if he intended to remain ; but to our surprise the next morning we found him gone. We were soon
in town and in less than an hour every house was in flames.
After leveling the works, a start was made again for Vicksburg, at which place we arrived on the 24th, where we went
into camp on the river bank just below the city.

There we remained resting until August 24th, when
we embarked on the steamer Fannie Bullet, which on the
25th started down the river and landed us four miles above
New Orleans two days later.

We remained here until September 25th, enjoying life
in the usual camp style, when we went to Donaldsonville,
returning to camp again on the 27th. October 3rd we took
a steamer for Algiers, and from here started on an expedition, going through Berwick City, Iberia and to Vermillion
Bay, where we went into camp on the 11th. October 15th
the march began again, went to "Carion Crow," Opolusas,
and stopped at Barris' Landing, where we remained until
November 1st. This was a march of over 100 miles. The
weather was scorching hot, the country a prairie with no
water, shade or vegetation. Water was carried in barrels
which had shafts attached to them, and turning over and
over, were drawn by horses or mules. A coil of wire on

the back of a mule and poles with sharp points to stick in the ground, furnished the material out of which a telegraph line was made, and in this way we had communication with the rest of the world, otherwise we were entirely cut off from civilization. The " Big five " could find nothing to take but sand, until the General found a cow one day, which was taken along for milking purposes, but on reaching camp soon disappeared and was seen no more alive.

We started back from here on November 1st, and on the 3rd, while at Grand Caton, were surprised by the enemy and almost bagged. The cavalry came swooping down upon us over the prairie and the infantry through the woods, drove us back until reenforcements came, which were just in time to save us. Our camp, baggage and everything was destroyed and burned, and out of a brigade of 1,200 men we had 700 wounded, killed and taken prisoners.

We now moved back to Iberia, which place we reached November 8th, and where we remained until December 7th, enjoying a needed rest and new blankets, for we had been without both from the date of our last engagement.

December 7th, the march was again taken up. Went through Franklin Berwick City, crossed Berwick Bay on the Steamer Starlight, disembarked, struck the Mississippi River about 55 miles above New Orleans, and moved on down till we reached Algiers.

This was a march of nearly 200 miles over a sandy country and when we reached our resting place on the 19th of December, we were glad enough. But orders soon came

to move and on the 22nd we took the Steamer Sallie Robinson and started for Fort Jackson, near the mouth of the Mississippi River. At the latter place, we remained in camp until January 28th, 1864, when we took a steamer for New Orleans, where we remained quartered in a cotton press until February 2nd.

From here we went to Lake Ponchertrain by rail and there took a steamer for Madisonville, where we arrived and disembarked on the 4th of February.

We left here on the 25th of February, going by cars, boat and on foot to New Orleans, Algiers, Brashier City, Franklin, Iberia, Vermillionville, Opelousas, Holmesville, Alaxandria, over Cane River, Nalchitochus, Pleasant Hill, and many other places, and not until April 8th, were we disturbed by the enemy. On that day, our regiment was guarding the ammunition train. The march began at 6 A. M., about noon heavy firing was heard in front and orders came for us to march at double quick to the scene of action. The train was long and our regiment, in order to guard it all, was of necessity long strung out. We were gotten together, the teams left in the rear, and for eight miles we kept up this march at quick time, hearing heavy firing all the time in our front. As soon as we reached the battle-ground, we formed in line on the extreme right of our army, at the same time supporting a battery. The battle soon became general all along the line. We were in an open field and soon had to fall back. The 3rd division came up to help, but they and we were swept back over the field by many times our number in the line of the enemy. Finally our army was forced back in great confusion, retreating over a half mile of open country. The

enemy was sure of a victory, but at last we found reenforcements in the 19th army corps, formed line with it,—and the enemy not being aware of our renewed and additional strength, rushed upon us as if the end had come and we were now all his. A tremendous volley was poured into their ranks, mowing them down like grain before the sickle. Thus they were broken up; they fell back. Both sides had struggled hard for the victory; neither had it; neither cared to renew the fight. A large number of men had been lost and nothing gained by either side. To us it was a surprise. We had been accustomed to driving everything before us; but not this time. At one time we were nearly cut off from the army and bagged. Wounded men walked all night to get to an ambulance. The drivers of these were compelled to cut loose their horses and flee for life, leaving the wagons and wounded on the field. Gen'l Ransom was shot; so was a number of other officers. We lost several pieces of artillery, and in all were badly crippled, but still in the field. Our regiment, though small in numbers at the time, lost 30 killed and wounded.

The next day we started back. Gen'l A. J. Smith, with the 19th army corps, had a hard fight with the enemy and repulsed him, taking back some of the guns lost the day previous. Our march was down Red River, through Grand Ecore, where we rested for a few days; then on April 21st crossed Cane River, went to " Henderson Hill." Alexandria, again, Fort Taylor, crossed the Atchafalaya River, by making a bridge over the bows of boats, which were run abreast clear across the river, then went on until we reached Morganza Bend on the Mississippi River, where we rested for seven days.

59

This march, lasting from April 9th to May 22nd, and consisting of about 200 miles traveled, was very fatigueing. The enemy kept close in our rear all the time, and hot skirmishing was indulged in daily. Several times we stopped long enough to throw up breastworks, but no stand was made by either side, and consequently no hard fighting done during the time. This was the end of the Red River Expedition. It had not been a success and the war would have ended just as soon, if it had never been conceived or carried out.

On the 28th of May we took the steamer Pioneer and were taken to Baton Rouge, La., where we remained in camp until July 21st. While here, foraging parties were frequent, and the "Big five" did a flourishing business. The teams would be sent far out into the country for corn, with parties sufficient to guard them. One of these excursions found a farm house where there was plenty of corn and chickens, and to the delight of the boys a good dinner just ready to serve, and several young ladies,—invited guests,—ready to sit down to it. The boys took seats at the table and ate all before them. The ladies were disgusted, but what could they do? This was only a sample of every day life while foraging for feed for man and beast, and a book could be written of the laughable incidents that grew out of these frequent visitations.

The boys would often bring in chickens and take them to town and sell them. To keep them all night was no easy matter. Some one would steal them almost to a certainty, unless they were watched. One of our boys brought in a large number from one of these excursions and in order to save them, tied a string to his foot, the

same being fast to his chickens. In this condition he went to sleep. The whole camp was awakened at midnight by the squalling of chickens and screams of a man. T'was the soldier and his chickens all going down the hill, together with two sturdy men as the motor power. The chickens went, the soldier stayed, regretting that he had slept. On July 21st our regiment embarked on the steamer Red Chief and dropped down to Algiers, opposite New Orleans, where we remained until the 26th, when we took the Alice Vivian and went to Morganza Bend, where we remained until September 12th with little to do. While here, however, we made several excursions into the country looking for bands of guerrillas. Sometimes we would find them, and much fierce skirmishing was indulged in, but nothing serious until October 19th, when we had a sharp fight of over three hours across the Atchafalaya, where several of our men were wounded. We finally returned to our camp on the 29th of October, and remained until October 31st. On th's last date, with other regiments, we took the boat for an up river expedition. We stop at all the principal points, march out into the country to find, if possible, the bands that are constantly firing into our boats, and making navigation unsafe. We continue this kind of warfare, making our home on the boats, until the 10th of December, when we go into camp at Natchez Here again the foraging parties went out nearly every day. We had lived well on chickens, pork, corn bread and molassas while on the boats, and were prepared to continue it now. The weather was cold, an allowance of wood was issued daily, but not enough to keep us warm. The Government had large piles near, which were guarded by day and night.

61

The soldiers were the guards, and the soldiers wanted the wood, safe to say the guards were not vigilant, and wood disappeared each night.

Here we stayed until January 28th, 1865. We spent Christmas and New Year doing camp duty and hoping for something better a year hence. On the 17th of January the 83rd and 48th O. V. I. were consolidated, all under the name of the 83rd. This caused great dissatisfaction among the members of the latter organization. But the soldier must learn to take what comes, he has no choice of his own, and the 48th boys had the sympathy of the 83rd, for they were doubtless as proud of their name, as we were of ours. January 28th, 1865, we embarked on the steamer Grey Eagle, which landed us at New Orleans on the 30th; here we took the cars for Lake Ponchertrain, at which place we embarked on the steamer Alabama—a captured vessel—and put out for Pensacola, Florida, landing at Barancas, just opposite the city, on the 1st of February.

There, are Forts Pickens and McKrea. O ir camp was beautified with evergreens, the weather mild, and withal we fared well until the 11th day of March, when we stored all our tents and other baggage in Fort Pickens and started on a march through a swampy, uninhabited country, reaching Pensacola the same afternoon, where we remained till March 20th. This city was almost ruined by the war; the population had fallen from 3000 to about 1500, all of whom were very poor. The enemy's works were very strong. Ditches about the forts were so arranged, that water could be turned in, in case of an attack.

From here we start for the interior. The 2nd division of the 13th army corps are all in line, each regiment is

allowed two wagons for all baggage, and no more, while we carried five day's rations in our haversacks. The weather is bad. It rains almost constantly. We almost carry the mules and wagons through the swamps and only march from two to five miles a day. Some days we cropped trees and made corduroy roads as we went, and when we rested at night would feel as if we had marched twenty miles, when in fact one or two would constitute the day's work. We hear of the enemy, but what he can be doing in this place we cannot divine; we credit him with more sense than to stay in such a place. We passed some forts and magazines, crossed the Tuscumbia and Perdido Rivers, and after a series of mishaps, arrived at Blakely on the 2nd of April, where we found the enemy in force and strongly fortified. We had now marched more than 100 miles over the worst roads and through the most God forsaken country I ever saw. Even the "Big Five" were disgusted. I still think it would have been good tactics to have let the enemy retain the full possession of that land of misery, for it was so poor and villainous, the men would soon have starved and saved us from killing them and being killed ourselves. It was actually a relief to find the enemy and accept the danger we were now confronted with, in place of what we had endured for several days past.

As above stated, we had neared the enemy's works, and now the fight was on. Our lines were formed about two miles from the fort, and slowly and cautiously we pressed forward, exchanging shots with our foe as we advanced upon him. At last we were so close that we began building earthworks for protection, and whenever the pickets made an advance movement at night, they took

pick and shovel with them, each digging his own hole
before day dawned. The enemy was very energetic in
throwing shot and shell into our quarters, and our battery,
directly in front of us, invited these responses in kind, and
made camp exceedingly unpleasant as a place to live. This
went on till April 9th, when it was learned Spanish Fort
had fallen. In the evening of that day we were called into
line and thence into our rifle pits without a moments
warning of what was coming. It was soon known however,
that a charge was to be made on the enemy's works.
Silently we stood, awaiting orders to go. We knew the
field in our front was planted with torpedoes and that our
way to the fort was beset with every impediment that
ingenuity and the evil one could invent. But go we must.
Soon one regiment from each brigade was detailed to go in
advance. It fell to our lot to take that position with reference to our brigade. A signal was to be given and we
were to climb out of the works and start. It soon came,
and in a moment a line two miles long was on its way to
the works and to victory. The regiments in reserve could
not be held back ; against orders they left the works and
started after us. On and on we went, until we reached the
enemy's works, and went right in, capturing everything he
had, even to his supper. As this was the last battle in
which we were engaged, and I believe the last of the war,
I will insert here a description of this charge, which was
written by a man on the field, and published at Mobile in
the office of the "*Daily News*," three days later, the type
being set by soldiers who took part in the fight :

Early Sunday morning, the 9th, General Steele, commanding the forces at this point, was made aware of the capture of Spanish Fort, although not officially, the fault not being that of General Canby, but elsewhere. It was unfortunate for the General, inasmuch as he *might* have made arrangements and dispositions that would have resulted in the capture of Blakely, earlier, even, than he did. It is not, however, a matter of importance, or a question to discuss, as events have transpired. Blakely is ours, and that is sufficient.

As I said, General Steele, learning of the capture of Spanish Fort, was early in the saddle and along the lines. The enemy opened in the morning, with their usual vim and activity, but about 10 o'clock almost entirely ceased firing the heavy guns, but keeping up a continual firing along their skirmish lines. Your correspondent visited the works of General C. C. Andrews, commanding the Second division, Thirteenth Army corps, which was stationed nearly in front of the center of the enemy's works, and had a fine opportunity (speaking in a military and not social sense) of seeing and learning the situation. The works of General Andrews were very extensive, and near enough those of his adversary to exchange compliments with weapons of the shortest range.

General Hawkins, commanding the colored divisions, was to the right of General Andrews and General Veatch, commanding 1st Division of Thirteenth Army Corps, to the left; General Garrard, of the 16th Army Corps, being

on the left still of General Veatch, and on the extreme
right of the enemy.

There was considerable skirmishing along the front
throughout the day (Sunday) and in the afternoon General
Steele consulted with General Canby, who had by this time
come up with the remainder of the Thirteenth and Six-
teenth Army Corps, and expressing his opinion that the
works could be carried, requested permission to strengthen
and advance his skirmish line, with the object of feeling
the enemy, and, if possible, entering their works, which
was finally decided on. General Steele at once ordered an
advance to be made along the entire line at half-past 5 P. M.
The skirmish line was accordingly strengthened and the
reserves brought up. It was soon generally known that an
advance was to be made, and there was of course no little
interest manifested.

THE ADVANCE.

About a quarter to 6 the guns along the line opened
fire, and the woods echo with their thunder, the air is filled
with smoke, the skirmishers fire more rapidly and advance
with a quicker step, and the enemy reply with volleys.
But the brave boys move on with no thought of turning
back, and now they are upon the double quick and nearing
rapidly the enemy's works, from which the balls come
flying thick and fast. On yet, and still on, until they are up

> " Into the very jaws of death,
> Into the very gates of hell."

Quicker, faster yet, through the almost impassable *abattis*,
up to the very embrasures from which come fire, and smoke
and death. Once an officer commanding cried out : " Down,

men," and of the many that did not hear or did not heed
the warning, but two were left standing. Grape and can-
nister had done their work, and many brave boys lay dead
and wounded. Up jumped the fortunate ones in another
instant; and now, see! they are up the works, and look!
there go the reserves after them on the run! Their officers
cannot keep them back, and they run on, deaf, as it were,
to order and ordnance. Hark! do you hear that cheer? It
is scarcely twenty minutes since our skirmishers advanced,
and now they are inside the works and their supporting
column are climbing the parapet in swarms! Who ever
saw a sight that surpassed that in point of bravery, alacrity
and determination? What is the result of that brief half
hour's work? The complete possession of the line of earthworks, bastions and forts, two and a half or three miles
long, strongly protected with a double line of *abattis* in
front, mounting some thirty guns and garrisoned by 3,000
men!

INSIDE THE WORKS

were our brave boys when I arrived, and capturing and
taking therefrom, and to the rear of our lines, prisoners by
the hundred. General Granger and staff, who arrived upon
the ground about the time the assault was made, were
riding along the road to the works just ahead of me, when
a Confederate soldier came up to the General and said:
"General, I am glad to see you; do you know me?" He
proved to be one of the employes of the General " in those
good old times," I believe, at Fort Laramie. A little further on we were cautioned by our men that there were
hundreds of torpedoes, or "sub terra shells," as the Con-
federates call them, (Hell's paving stones, as I call them).

planted all about, and we reined up for a moment. Yes, we were on the shell road to Mobile, true enough! A moment later we met a batch of prisoners going to the rear under a guard, and the General ordered that they "should show where they were, or march over them."

When we arrived at the main works, the men were busy taking care of the prisoners and supplying themselves with ammunition, cartridges, cartridge boxes, bayonets, guns, etc., lying around in any quantity.

It was now dusk, and growing dark fast, but the garrison was searched out, and man after man captured in the woods and sent in with the rest.

RETURNING FROM THE WOODS

I saw some dead and many wounded, wearing the gray as well as the blue uniform, lying around. They did not lie long, however, for our ambulances were soon upon the ground, and the wounded of both alike conveyed to the hospitals. The dead were buried, and the mounds of earth with a stick or rude slab, mark the spot where repose brave men who not long since were friends, and breathed under the same banner, now buried where they so gallantly fought, and fighting, fell. They are enemies no longer.

To-day, as near as I can gather, the number of prisoners captured, number in the aggregate to over 3,000, although General Cockrell, who commanded the Missourians, and who is also a prisoner, stated that the entire garrison was only 2,400. General Garrard captured about 1,400, General Veatch, 400, General Hawkins about 300, and General Andrews about 1,300, including 71 commissioned officers, which will make, in all, 3,200 or 3,300.

68

This is as near as can be given at the present writing. The number of commissioned officers captured by the other divisions I can not state. There are among them several Colonels and Generals Cockrell and Thomas, and General Liddell, commanding the forces.

OTHER CAPTURES.

A large and valuable amount of war dispatches and correspondence and telegraphic dispatches, 50 beeves, 75 sheep, and large quantities of commissary stores were captured. There was tobacco, corn and meal, "hard tack," hams, salt, sugar, molasses, vinegar, etc. A good haul.

WHO WERE THE FIRST IN THE WORKS?

This is a much mooted question, and has perplexed me much to know how to answer in our columns. Where the line of works was so long, and where every division, brigade, regiment, company and man tried so hard and did so well, it is impossible to tell where the mantle should fall. The 83d Ohio, in General Andrews' front, and the 8th Illinois, in General Veatch's front, were there as soon as any, to say the least. The former, I believe it was, had two flagstaffs shot away; but the flags were picked up and planted on the works. The 76th Illinois was also very prompt and active, and did some hard fighting, as did the others. Nine of their men fell in a small space of a few yards square, right up by the enemy's works. Some of this regiment ordered a captain to surrender, which he refused to do, and, drawing his revolver, shot one of them, after the works were surrendered. He was shot down, and two of his men by his side, and the three now repose in one grave on the spot, inside the works, but a few steps from

the graves of the brave nine of the 76th Illinois. In
another place lay twenty-four killed and wounded.

Other regiments have also lost heavily. The skirmishers advanced along the roads leading to the fort, and after
getting within one hundred and fifty yards of the fort the
fire of musketry, grape and canister was such that almost
any troops would have turned and fled. These men did;
but they only turned from the roads which were being
swept with a murderous fire on the sides of them, and fled
in the direction of the forts and bastions, and actually
crawled through the embrasures while the cannon vomited
forth fire, smoke and death. The men did all and "dared
all that would become a man," and the day is ours. All
share in the glory, and did well—none did ill.

PERSONAL.

The capture of Blakely by Major General Steele's
forces will figure in history as one of *the* events of the war.
Major General Canby wrote a congratulatory letter to General Steele, in which he said, "God bless you and your
brave command."

TORPEDOES.

Another point I can not restrain my pen upon: That
torpedoes have been planted in the roads and approaches to
this place, as well as Spanish Fort, is well known. Of the
legitimacy or illegitimacy of this mode of defensive warfare of course, not being a military man, it is not for me to
decide. I have my own ideas (it's a wonder, after riding
around so much among these cursed inventions, that I have
any, or a head for them), and those ideas are of little or
no consequence to any one other than myself, but looks

to me as being an inhuman, barbarous and cowardly business, and if I had the power I would make every man who
put them down walk over them.

It is argued that they are as legitimate as mines. Let
us see about that : A mine is always under the control of
the operators before and after a surrender : if it is exploded
it only weakens or destroys an enemy. These torpedoes
are planted in every direction indiscriminately. Even the
enemy who put them down can not to-day go and dig them
all up, were they so disposed. They can not even enable ·
others to do so.

Well, the works are surrendered, and the prisoners of
war, as such, have no more to do with warfare so far as this
single contest goes. They have surrendered themselves and
their weapons of warfare, and the battle is ended. Have
they any right, moral, legal or military (any way you please).
to make war or kill further? What are the results? The
men, Mr. Editor and readers, who have braved the Minie
ball and the bursting shell, the solid shot and the grape and
canister; these men who bravely and heroically walked up
to the very muzzles of the enemy's guns and met their foes
face to face, and yet by a miracle, perhaps, escaped the terrific slaughter of a bloody assault, start back for their quarters, after having won the day, and are blown to pieces by
these damnable and hellish machines. More, some of those
that were on the humane and Christian task of assisting
and caring for our wounded were killed. One instance I
know of where the ambulances with the wounded from the
field were blown to atoms. The instances are numerous
where men who had lived unharmed through the deadly
strife, and gallantly stood up and met a visible danger, are

maimed for life by these unseen missiles. "Where is thy thunder, Heaven?" Months, and even, perhaps, years hence, when the war shall have ceased, and men, who once were friends, now foes shall be friends again; when the thunder of hostile cannon shall no more disturb our slumbers, when the grass shall be growing over these earthworks (monuments of men's passions), and the husbandmen shall go forth to sow his seed and reap his harvest within their inclosure, the same fair form which man should protect and cherish, some innocent, prattling child at play, may wake the sleeping demon, dull slumbering in the earth, and the tale of anguish that shall ensue no tongue nor pen describe. This is no fancy picture drawn from the imaginative and fertile brain. If you think so, reader, or you are disposed to argue or jest or laugh the thing away, come with me and see the misery, uncalled for, unnecessary, unhallowed, that they have caused. If that does not suffice, why walk over them yourself, and that *will*.

INCIDENTAL.

It is stated on authority above question, and which I would not dispute, that the enemy fired a volley of musketry into the bosom of our men after they were in the works, and those works surrendered. I am sorry to record this, and wish it were otherwise. But that they did fall back from their breastworks to the woods and fire as stated has been stated and proven to me so conclusively that it is beyond a doubt the fact. There I leave this matter.

Colonel Spurling, of the 2nd Maine Cavalry, now given a brigade by General Canby, which he is commanding, has performed many gallant exploits. One of them is this: He was among the first to enter the works with the troops,

and did not stop at the line, but went on to the landing at
Blakely, on the way to which he captured a mule, all sad-
dled and bridled. Mounting, he rode down and found a
rebel gunboat just leaving the wharf. The Captain was on
deck, and Colonel Spurling, raising his carbine to his shoulder, ordered the Captain to surrender. Seeing this persua-
sive instrument leveled at his head, in the hands of a man
who is a notorious deadshot, the Captain said, " I surrender." " Come ashore, then." " I will, sir." And the Captain started down the gangway, as the Colonel supposed,
for his small boat, but when he got down where he was
safe, ordered steam to be put on, and got away. It was a
very novel idea, that, however, one man ordering a gunboat
to surrender.

General Steele also captured a mule and, having left
his horse in the rear, took the mule along and rode to
camp. His orderly coming up and finding him in camp,
spoke of his horse, when the General said he "got along
very well; he rode upon a brevet horse."

OUR LOSSES.

The returns not being yet all in, it is impossible to
give the loss in the assault. It will not exceed, in killed
and wounded, 1,000. The 8th Illinois lost in a few minutes 64 killed and wounded; the 11th Wisconsin Veterans,
Colonel Whittlessey's regiment, 44 out of 400, two-thirds
of the loss of the entire Third Brigade. Colonel Harris
commanded this brigade, which is in General Garrard's
Division.

73

BLAKELY.

On the ninth of April, sixty-five,
　　Long remember'd be the day,
In range of Blakely's batteries
　　General Canby's forces lay;
They had waded sloughs and marshes,
　　Been exposed to winds and rain,
Marched o'er concealed torpedoes
　　This proximity to gain.

For here, within their stronghold,
　　Dreading an open field,
Had convened Dick Taylor's forces
　　To keep us from Mobile;
We tried their works with light guns,
　　But of these they did make sport,
Saying with such, it would take five years
　　And six months to take their fort.

Our good General, not wishing
　　To besiege their works so long,
Gave orders that assault be made
　　And carry them by storm;
Evening came on—at half-past five
　　Was the appointed time;
Our reserves were then moved to the front,
　　And formed in battle-line.

Our artillery opened on their works,
　　Their virtue thought to try,
When they opened their embrasures
　　And gave us a reply,
Dropping shot and shell around us,
　　Cutting branches o'er our heads,
While their leaden missiles thick and fast
　　On deadly errands sped.

Our skirmishers along the line
　　Engaged them—meanwhile
Our outward line was forming,
　　Preparing for the trial;
Our batteries then opened,
　　Using guns both small and large,
And command was given round the lines,
　　Battalions, Forward! Charge!

74

O, it was a glorious sight to see
　The gallantry displayed
Along the line of Union forces
　When that fearful charge was made;
Dashing forward o'er obstructions,
　Breasting a murderous fire
From which troops less determined
　In confusion would retire.

Onward, rushing to the muzzle
　Of huge death-dealing guns,
Each vieing to be foremost,
　And cheering as they run;
Mounting the rebel ramparts
　With shouts they rend the air,
And plant the " Emblem of the Free,"
　Our gloriour colors, there.

Three thousand Southern soldiers
　And many heavy guns
Are trophies of the victory
　Which this day has been won;
But these first fruits of our conquest
　Many never lived to see;
They perished in the conflict—
　Peace to their memory be.

A tear will glisten in the eye
　When comrades shall recite
The story of the struggle,
　How they fell amid the fight;
EIGHTH ILLINOIS! brave regiment!
　Lost heavily to-day,
Being deployed as skirmishers,
　They were foremost in the fray.

The ELEVENTH behaved gallantly,
　As is their wont to do;
They understand the business
　Of putting rebels through;
The colors of the OLD FORTY-SIXTH,
　Borne on despite of balls,
Were among the first that floated
　Triumphant o'er the walls.

75

Nine or ten men of the SEVENTY-SIXTH
    Dead on one spot did lay;
The EIGHTY-THIRD OHIO
    Had two flagstaffs shot away;
The TWENTIETH IOWA, luckily,
    Lost not a single man,
Though early on the rebel works
    Their colors took a stand;
Of other troops I can not speak,
    Yet know they all fought well—
The story of their valor
    Future history will tell.
How at Blakely, under ANDREWS,
    CARR, VEATCH, GARRARD, HAWKINS, STEELE,
They won a victory which gave them
    The City of Mobile.

How, upon the 12th, they crossed the bay,
    Took possession of the town,
And into quiet camp-life
    They once more settled down;
Here we will leave them, but I fear
    That eyes of softest blue
Will do what Southern armed men
    Have essayed in vain to do,
And many, many a Northern maid
    May yet deep anguish feel,
Should her lover fall a victim
    To some "Fair Rebel" in Mobile.

The above gives a faint description of what took place
that evening. What was done in the works before starting,
the feeling of the men who were about to take their lives
in their hands, the charge itself, can not be described, but
all these must live in the imagination of those who never
experienced an hour in which so much history was made,
and so many lives lost.

Six killed and twenty-four wounded comprised the list
of the 83d. Other regiments suffered a greater loss. Both
of our flagstaffs were cut in two by bullets, but the flags
were planted on the works.

76

The next day is one of sorrow. We are burying the dead, writing letters home to tell of the awful scene, and caring for the wounded, while squads of rebel prisoners are out digging up the torpedoes which were intended for us. On the 11th of April we moved into Blakely and remained there until the 20th, when we took the steamer Gen. Cowles and went over to Mobile, from which place we start the same evening with a fleet consisting of thirteen transports, one monitor and one man of war, for Selma, Ala., which place we reached April 27th, and there went into camp and stayed until May 12th.

Leaving Selma we came back to Mobile and remained there until June 13th, when we took a steamer for Galveston, Texas. Our voyage by sea was unpleasant, and the worst of all was that we laid just outside of the harbor for two days, the ship rolling and tossing, waiting for high tide and a pilot to take us in. Once in that city our hard times were over. We ate, drank, bathed and slept from now until July 24th, when we were ordered into line and mustered out of the United States service under Special Order 84, 13th Army Corps. Eighteen days were allowed us to get to Camp Dennison, Ohio, where we would receive our last pay, turn over our guns and go home.

We left Galveston, Texas, July 26th, on the steamer Livingston, which landed us in New Orleans July 28th. On the 29th took passage on the Henry Ames and started for Cairo, which place we reached on the 3d of August, leaving by rail the next day. We arrived in Cincinnati about 11 o'clock on the night of the 5th, went to Camp Dennison the next day, and were paid and finally discharged and permitted to go home August 10th, 1865. Many that were with us when we left were not there when we returned. This thought alone marred the joy and pleasures of that day.